"The bandits obviously robbed the train seventy years ago for the fortune carried aboard it. Very few of those stolen goods have ever shown up, and the gold bullion never did." He paused. "Some say that treasure has never left Blackpool.

"Maybe, ladies and gentlemen, maybe we'll be the ones to find out what happened to all those valuables seventy years ago. Maybe we'll find out who robbed that train and killed those people so callously."

The double doors leading into the theater suddenly banged open. A rectangle of fluorescent light from the lobby fell into the room. A woman stood silhouetted in the doorway.

"Inspector Paddington!"

"Here." Paddington heaved himself up and whipped a torch from his equipment belt. He snapped it on and a bright blue-white beam shot out.

The woman in the doorway flinched, shielding her eyes with one hand. The inspector's light revealed the blood spread across her fingers and wrist. "Come quick. There's been a murder."

Cast of Characters

Michael and Molly Graham—The young couple have come to Blackpool for a simpler life...only things in the small town are anything but simple.

Iris Dunstead—The elderly housekeeper knows everyone and everything that happens in town. But with so many pokers in the fire, is she in for a bad burn?

DCI Paddington—The stolid inspector has a laid-back approach to investigation—so laid-back that it's fueled rumors he's only in Blackpool to bide his time until retirement.

Simon Wineguard—The recent behavior of the director of Molly's documentary suggests he could be the subject of an exposé himself.

Synthia Roderick—With the nickname of Syn and the lifestyle to support it, her sudden appearance in a small coastal town is very suspicious....

Joyce Abernathy—The responsible and organized assistant of Simon Wineguard, her motto seems to be "always the assistant, never the bride." It doesn't seem to bother her... or does it?

The Crowes—The members of the Crowe family are reputed to have more secrets than they have money. And they keep both very well.

The Sterlings—Another wealthy family whose name keeps coming up around the train robbery. The family lost a fortune and a child that day. Seventy years later, justice has yet to be served.

Greed, jealousy, betrayal, trickery, murder—Blackpool is a town built on secrets and danger.

MYSTERY CASE FILES

Stolen

A BLACKPOOL MYSTERY

Jordan Gray

HARLEQUIN®

1017

TORONTO • NEW YORK • LONDON
AMSTERDAM • PARIS • SYDNEY • HAMBURG
STOCKHOLM • ATHENS • TOKYO • MILAN • MADRID
PRAGUE • WARSAW • BUDAPEST • AUCKLAND

Recycling programs
for this product may
not exist in your area.

ISBN-13: 978-0-373-83751-9

STOLEN

Copyright © 2010 by Harlequin Books S.A.

Special thanks and acknowledgment to Mel Odom for his
contribution to this work.

Big Fish Games logo and Mystery Case Files logos are trademarks or
registered trademarks of Big Fish Games, Inc.

Printed in U.S.A.

CHAPTER ONE

"Looks like everyone in town showed up." Michael Graham peered through the tinted window of his vintage limousine at the crowd gathered in front of the Magic Lantern Theatre. Chinese-style lanterns in bright colors hung over the marquee that announced, "Special Announcement Plus Showing of *Peter Pan 2: Return to Neverland*."

"That was the point." Molly leaned in over her husband's shoulder.

For a moment, Michael grew distracted by her perfume and the heat of her body pressing against his. They'd been married three years, but her sheer physical presence still made a tremendous impact on his senses. He knew that would never change, and he was glad for it. He grinned in spite of himself and kissed the back of her neck.

Molly shivered, as he knew she would, and pulled back. She held up a forefinger in warning. "Don't even think about that."

Michael laughed, but he let her have her space and returned his attention to the festivities filling downtown Blackpool. His newly adopted town was still fascinating to him and constantly inspired his creative juices. The mixture of old and new strewn throughout the hills and up to the cliffs overlooking the sea enthralled him.

Normally on a Friday night, Blackpool's streets remained relatively desolate. Truly there wasn't much to do in town. Most of the action took place out on the sea, or on the beaches where the teens met up to drink out of sight of their parents.

But tonight the throng gathered all along the police barricade in front of the movie house, filling the thoroughfare and making traffic all but impossible. A few people slapped the limousine or waved as it passed. Not everyone in Blackpool knew the Grahams, but all of them had heard of them.

And even without the limo they would have stood out. Most Blackpoolers walked or biked as the narrow streets downtown and twisty switchbacks up the hills made driving impractical. Tourists and visitors usually arrived by boat and tied up in the harbor.

But the limo had come with the house they'd purchased when moving to Blackpool, and Irwin Jaeger—the houseman—had come with both. They seldom used the car, which often disappointed Irwin.

Tonight the black night was fought off by more streetlights than normal, illuminating the squat stone-and-wood buildings in the town square. The brightness seemed out of place amid warehouses and shops more than a century old.

Still focused on her iPhone, Molly Graham shot Michael a quick glance. "I'm glad to see you're finally back among the living and not off robbing crypts or fighting orcs or goblins."

Chagrined, Michael set aside his small netbook. Partially drafted monsters filled the tiny screen. A pang of guilt twisted within him. "Sorry, love. Didn't mean to go away on you these past few days right before your event."

"I can't blame you." Molly glanced through the window and frowned. "I was distracted by last-minute details." Her dark auburn hair curled under and swept her bare shoulders. The understated black dress showed off her petite figure but maintained an air of professionalism. A black onyx set in a silver pendant hung at the hollow of her throat from a fine silver chain.

Michael understood her distraction. His profession as a video and computer game designer demanded unwavering focus, as well. Molly's work in public relations and grant writing consumed her from time to time, as well, especially since she assumed responsibilities on her project for beyond what was required, or what she got credit for. She didn't hold back, and that passion was only one of the reasons he loved her so much.

"Of course you do."

Molly lifted an arched brow. "You were distracted by mermaids."

Michael chuckled. "No more than usual. And, in my defense, mermaids can be quite distracting."

"I've seen the drawings of mermaids your illustrator friend, Keith, sent you. Not exactly Disney, I must say."

Michael chuckled. "Well, Keith's a naughty boy. And it gets toned down for the market."

Molly leaned in and kissed him. Her warm lips lingered on his for a moment and tasted like cherries. She drew back and looked directly at him. "The netbook stays in the car when we go inside."

Michael grimaced. Molly straightened the collar and lapels of his thigh-length black leather jacket. "I need you to be yourself tonight."

"I'm always myself."

"True, but tonight I need the emphasis put on the wonderful and adorable self."

Michael rolled his eyes in mock reproach. "You want arm candy."

"You can let people know you have a brain."

"Ah. Thank God for that."

The limousine rolled a few more feet toward the theater, mired in the crowd. On the other side of the privacy screen, Irwin Jaeger shook his head. He thumbed a button that rolled the glass down and glanced in the rearview mirror.

"My apologies. It appears we won't get any closer tonight despite my best efforts."

Neatly cut iron-gray hair lay under the chauffeur's cap he'd put on for fun and a bushy mustache covered his upper lip. Thick bifocal lenses made his muddy-brown eyes look larger than normal. The tailored livery fit his thin frame exactly.

"This will be fine, Irwin." Molly smiled at the old man.

"Very good, ma'am." With an economy of movement, Irwin put the transmission in Park, got out and came around the car, opening the door with a flourish.

"Thank you, Irwin." Michael climbed out, then extended a hand to Molly. She reached back into the car for a black wrap. Michael draped it over her shoulders, then guided her toward the crowd in front of the theater.

In the distance, Michael noticed Glower Lighthouse standing tall over Blackpool. Even when fog shrouded it and the light appeared to stab out of nowhere, the place seemed threatening, and seeing it at night chilled Michael. During the day, he experienced nothing out of the ordinary, but when he went to the lighthouse at night, especially with the local group of cave explorers he sometimes accompanied, he definitely felt something unsettling lingering in the timbers and stone. And he didn't believe in ghosts. At least, not much.

Michael smiled as the crowd surrounded Molly and him. It was her night, and he wanted to watch her bask in the event she'd brought to life. He trailed along a step behind her, referring everyone who had questions to Molly.

CONFRONTED BY DOZENS of people, Molly Graham felt as though she'd stepped into her element. She loved being on stage, loved being the center of attention, and she loved bringing a production to successful fruition—in this case the filming of a documentary right here in Blackpool. Her senses suddenly seemed sharper, her thoughts clearer, and strength coursed through her. To her, public relations was a kaleidoscope of pure energy.

"Mrs. Graham, you've managed to pull off quite the little event here. Will you give us a hint of anything special you've planned?" Fred Purnell, reporter for the local paper, straightened one of his suspenders over his broad belly and forced his way next to Molly. His thinning hair lay oiled against his scalp and he wore his best shirt.

Molly smiled, conscious of the teen photographer that trailed Fred. The girl had a death grip on her camera. The flash went off and temporarily blinded Molly. She never missed a step as she listened to the dozens of curious voices around her.

"Patience, Mr. Purnell." Molly plowed through the crowd, and the reporter struggled to keep up.

Purnell grimaced. "Everyone in town wants to know if you've discovered anything more about the robbery."

"All in due time."

"C'mon, Molly. Give an aging newspaperman a break. If you'd written a press release, I could have already filed this story for the *Journal*."

Purnell was a dogged reporter for the newspaper he owned and operated, the *Blackpool Journal,* when news was breaking, but things were often slow in Blackpool. Except for the mystery surrounding Ravenhearst Manor and poor Emma Ravenhearst. He ran stories concerning the family whenever he could because they often got picked up by larger newspapers.

"What about the robbery? Molly, for God's sake."

Glancing over her shoulder, Molly spotted Michael a half step behind her. A devilish smile curved his lips at Purnell's remonstrations.

Although she'd looked at her husband countless times, she could never grow tired of it. There was something earthy and magnetic about him, about the smooth way he moved. She had to admit, the leather jacket looked great on him, projecting a raw, rugged image that suited him well. He wore a black turtleneck under it and black slacks. At six feet two inches tall, he kept his black hair shaved almost to the scalp, and his carefully trimmed goatee made him look distinguished.

Michael mouthed the word, *Robbery?*

Molly grinned impishly at him.

Everybody loved a mystery. Her uncle Peter, who worked for the Mystery Case Files Agency, an international private investigation firm, had regaled her with stories of crimes and criminals since she was a girl. She'd hung on his every word and loved trying to solve the crimes he'd dangled before her.

Most people had heard rumors about the documentary and knew that it was connected to an infamous robbery. But no one knew all the details. To make things even more exciting, this was a mystery that even she didn't have all the answers to. And, of course, there was the treasure. The lure of it would draw a lot of interest.

The answers would surely follow.

CHAPTER TWO

"YOU KNOW, MRS. GRAHAM. I really don't think this is such a good idea. Didn't think so to begin with, and I like it even less now."

Detective Chief Inspector Maurice Paddington of the Blackpool Police Department raked a scarred knuckle across the thick shelf of his jaw and shook his shaggy head. His trench coat was rumpled and he held his unlit pipe in his hand. In his fifties and overweight, Paddington nevertheless remained a bulldog when it came to law enforcement.

At the moment, he stood solidly behind one of the police sawhorses blocking entrance to the theater. He was as much a bulwark as the sawhorse and the police officers around him.

Occasionally the Blackpool Police Department pulled in smugglers and drug runners who tried to do business in town, and sometimes they arrested thieves and vandals, but the town didn't have much in the way of criminal activity. Now, anyway—as a former pirate den, it had a history of outlaws. But Paddington kept the current peace with a heavy hand and simple, inflexible rules.

The police department only had a small contingent of officers, but more had been drafted to help manage security for the filming of the documentary Molly was going to announce tonight.

Molly stood waiting for one of the police officers to

remove the sawhorse blocking her path. "It's a little late to stop this now, don't you think?"

Paddington squinted at her, harrumphed and turned away. He waved at one of the young officers standing nearby. "Let Mr. and Mrs. Graham pass, Constable Bedford."

The young policeman eased the sawhorse away, allowed Molly and Michael through, then pushed the barrier back into place to control the rest of the crowd.

TWENTY-SEVEN MINUTES LATER, Molly stood to one side of the Magic Lantern's large screen. For the moment the houselights glowed dimly and served only to stir the darkness inside the large room. Townsfolk filled every seat.

"You appear to have quite the turnout, Mrs. Graham."

Barely managing to quash an involuntary start, Molly turned toward the smooth, oily voice.

Aleister Crowe stood there in elegant evening wear. In his early thirties and with his dark hair worn brushed back to reveal a widow's peak, he looked as predatory as his namesake. Light reflected from the silver crow's head topping the walking stick he carried purely for looks, though rumor held that it was a sword cane passed down through generations of Crowes.

"I do hope you can deliver on all the furor you promised." Crowe's voice was controlled and deep, an orator's voice. "Even if you do, though, I doubt the detective chief inspector will be very pleased with you. You're threatening the orderliness he works so hard to maintain in Blackpool."

Breathing out slowly, Molly chose to be calm and collected. Something about Crowe and his family always left her feeling on edge. Aleister had come into his own after his father had mysteriously died at sea a dozen years ago.

"On the contrary, Mr. Crowe, I believe Inspector Paddington will be happy after tonight's announcement. His department is going to get a good deal of publicity during the filming of the documentary."

Shifting his attention, Crowe gazed at the seated crowd and those standing at the back of the theater.

"For such a small town, Blackpool seems to attract huge secrets. It would be a shame if you tripped across something that had been buried for a long time while seeking to film your little movie." He shrugged. "You might want to consider that before you start kicking a hornet's nest."

"Is that a warning, Mr. Crowe?"

He smiled, and a neutral expression slipped across his face like a well-used mask. "Not at all. Just an objective observation."

"As I understand it, the Crowe family has no shortage of buried secrets." They'd lived in Blackpool since the first pirates and smugglers had lit campfires on the seashores. "Is this documentary going to touch on one?"

"Touché, my dear." Crowe drained his wineglass and placed it on the tray of a passing server. He shrugged and glanced around the room. "I suppose I should mingle and leave you to your event."

"I hope you enjoy the evening."

Crowe nodded, then turned and walked away, disappearing almost instantly in the darkness of the theater.

Creepy. Molly shook her head and promised herself that she wouldn't tell Michael about the encounter. He thought Crowe was obnoxious, but not scary. Threatening, maybe, but not supernatural. Molly wasn't so certain. There was something menacing about Aleister Crowe—about all of the Crowes, actually—and Molly couldn't quite shake it off. Maybe it was just the eeriness of Blackpool itself. The stories continued to cycle about infamous resident Emma

Ravenhearst and the ghost that was said to haunt the ruins
of where the old Ravenhearst mansion had stood just outside town.

At precisely seven o'clock, Molly walked out onto center
stage. The baby spotlight switched on with a loud *snap* and
bathed her in blue-white incandescence. She kept from
blinking through an effort of will and avoided looking into
the light. She couldn't see the audience, but she heard a
hush falling over the crowd, receding from the stage like
an outgoing tide.

"Good evening, ladies and gentlemen and children."
Molly spoke naturally and the wireless mic pinned to her
top carried her voice to the back of the theater. "I want to
thank you all for coming." She smiled.

Michael sat in the front row beside Fred Purnell. The
chair to Michael's left was empty, as were a couple of
others. Simon Wineguard, the documentary's director, wasn't seated where he was supposed to be and that
bothered Molly. They'd agreed about the timing and the
seating.

"We're here to honor seven survivors of the Blackpool
train robbery that occurred in 1940. We'll have those people
on stage shortly. But as you've probably heard around town,
that isn't the only reason for this event. To explain, please
join me in welcoming Simon Wineguard, the famed director and historian." Molly glanced at the empty seat in the
front row. "Simon, are you out there?"

"Over here, Molly."

The voice came from Molly's left. A moment later, the
director trotted across the stage to stand beside her. In his
forties, Wineguard was tall and a little overweight. His
suit hung well on him, working with the rimless glasses to
give him a professional appearance. He was bald on top,
his shiny pate fringed by short salt-and-pepper hair.

He hugged Molly briefly.

"Sorry, my dear. I lost track of time and ended up not being where I was supposed to be when I was supposed to be there." Despite his outward calm, Wineguard seemed a little flustered. Maybe he was nervous about all the attention. He was used to being behind a camera.

"I knew I should have given you a map."

"And maybe a keeper," called out a feminine voice from the front row.

Wineguard gave the crowd a mock grimace and offered a wave to the front row. "That would be Joyce Abernathy, my personal assistant."

A petite woman in her middle years stood and waved to the audience. Short gray hair accentuated her broad features. Over the last few weeks, Molly had gotten to know Joyce well and thought she was a fantastic little dynamo to work with.

"If his mother were here, Simon would have been in his seat."

The crowd roared with laughter.

"Yes, well, thank you for that, Joyce." Wineguard shook his head and looked insufferably put upon as Joyce sat back down.

Molly loved that Wineguard and Joyce worked so well together. It made selling this project much easier to do.

"Many of you have probably heard of Simon," Molly said to return the focus to where it should be—the announcement of the documentary. "He's directed several history specials that have aired on the BBC, Discovery Channel and the History Channel. His films have been translated into more than thirty languages."

"Thankfully, I didn't have to learn all of them."

The crowd laughed again, but this time there were a

few jeers, as well. If the director heard them, he gave no indication.

"Some of Simon Wineguard's more well-known pieces include *Blackout Nights,* a history of London during World War II. *Spies Among England's Gentry,* concerning wealthy British families torn apart by that war. And *Constables Chasing Swastikas,* a documentary of London's Metropolitan Police Department pursuing black-market dealers during wartime."

As she spoke, footage trailed across the screen behind her.

"Mr. Wineguard has come to Blackpool, to *you,* to follow up on another story." Molly let her words hang and the interest build. "When the Second World War began, the government decided to move women and children outside of the metropolitan areas to protect them. London and the other major cities were prime targets for German bombs."

Silence hung over the crowd. Although the war was seventy years ago, public interest and memory had not diminished. Several London neighborhoods still bore scars of the bombing. No one had forgotten.

"That decision led to Operation Pied Piper."

The footage on the screen changed, showing black-and-white reels of actual evacuations of the English cities. Tearful women and children were herded onto waiting trains like cattle.

Simon Wineguard stepped forward slightly. "I can't imagine what it was like to be loaded onto a train and not know if I'd ever see my dad again. To watch bombs being dropped into your city, perhaps right outside your window, and then you're shipped away from your dad. Maybe your mum, too."

The audience watched the black-and-white reels in rapt silence.

"Pied Piper has always fascinated me but I didn't think I could do anything new with the subject." Wineguard shoved his hands into his slacks pockets and walked away from Molly. The baby spotlight followed him and left her in the darkness. The move had been planned and everyone looked at him. "However, I found an interesting story while pursuing research on this special little hobby of mine."

Molly sensed the anticipation building among the crowd. Fred Purnell leaned forward in his seat with his digital recorder outstretched. His teen photographer flashed away and bright light illuminated the stage again and again.

"Imagine my surprise when I discovered that Blackpool had served as a final destination for some of those displaced families." Sheer excitement widened Wineguard's smile. "And in 1940, some of those evacuees were on a train when it was derailed just outside of Blackpool. Not only that, but some of the children aboard that train remained in Blackpool and made this lovely town their home. Seven of those children live in Blackpool to this day."

A montage of seven faces, four male and three female, replaced the previous images of evacuees. There were pictures of the survivors as children as well as adults.

"These people will be joining us in just a few moments." Wineguard waved to the photographs on the screen. "We're going to honor them, watch *Peter Pan 2,* then attend a small buffet."

A spattering of clapping started and briefly gained momentum. Wineguard raised his hands to quiet it. Molly relaxed a little. Perhaps there wouldn't be as much resistance to the intrusion and publicity as she'd feared. Blackpool and its citizens were hard to judge.

"But before we do that, I want to take just a couple

more minutes to tell you what I'm going to be doing here. What *we're* going to be doing over the next few weeks." Wineguard paused. "Thanks to Molly Graham's brilliant grant application and vision, I've received funding to do a documentary based on Blackpool's connection to Operation Pied Piper. In fact, I think I've got quite the hook for our little enterprise."

Well played. Moving it from my *to* our. Molly watched the man with increasing admiration. She'd been impressed by the director when she'd first met him, but that appreciation grew tremendously tonight.

Wineguard's voice lowered as if he was taking the whole audience into his confidence. "As you all know, the derailment of 1940 wasn't an accident. It was a robbery." He let the audience hang on to his words for just a moment. "The train carried several women and children evacuating from London, including an heir to the Sterling family fortune. Sadly, little Chloe Sterling perished when the bandits blew the train off its tracks."

The image behind Wineguard switched to the scene of a train wreck. An overturned locomotive lay across the tracks in front of a shamble of broken cars. Groups of people clustered around trees and boulders with dazed, shocked expressions. Others lay on the ground under blankets.

Several women in the audience shook their heads. A few crossed themselves.

"Who would do such a thing? I'm sure you've all asked that question at one time or another." Wineguard spread his hands wide. "Sadly, the military police never found the malefactors behind this tragic deed."

"What monster would wreck that train with all those kids on it? And why?" The question came from somewhere in the back of the room.

Wineguard looked out into the crowd as if he could see

the man who'd spoken. "Exactly my question. That train also carried a fortune in art, jewelry and pottery. All from collections of wealthy families who were afraid to leave such treasures behind in London. More than that, there was a shipment of gold bullion on board marked for the war effort."

More whispers circulated the theater.

"The bandits obviously robbed the train for its valuable cargo." Wineguard shrugged. "They didn't care how much death and suffering they caused."

He scanned the audience. "Very few of those stolen goods have ever shown up. And the gold bullion never did." He walked to the edge of the stage. "Some say that treasure—perhaps even the paintings—was sorted out, sold to private collectors who will never show their ill-gotten gain to anyone." He paused, holding everyone's attention. "But…some say that treasure has never left Blackpool."

For a moment, the auditorium was completely silent. Then a few whispered comments and questions broke the stillness. The volume of voices rose, and Wineguard stood in the spotlight rubbing his hands.

"Maybe, ladies and gentlemen, maybe we'll be the ones to find out what happened to all those valuables seventy years ago. Maybe we'll find out who robbed that train and killed those people so callously. At the very least, I hope we open a fresh avenue of investigation."

The double doors leading into the theater suddenly banged open. A rectangle of fluorescent light from the lobby fell into the room. A woman stood silhouetted in the doorway.

"Inspector Paddington!"

"Here." Paddington heaved himself up and whipped a torch from his equipment belt. He snapped it on and a bright blue-white beam shot out.

The woman in the doorway flinched, shielding her eyes
with one hand. The inspector's light revealed the blood
spread across her fingers and wrist.

"Come quick," she urged. "There's been a murder."

CHAPTER THREE

MURDER! THE WORD FLOWED through the theater audience like quicksilver.

Michael heaved up from his seat with the intention of going to Molly. But by the time he got to his feet, several panicked theatergoers had filled the aisles, blocking his way. To make matters worse, Molly didn't stay on the stage. Instead, she somehow scrambled down and managed to tuck herself in neatly at Paddington's heels. A couple of policemen flanked her.

Michael ground his teeth as he pushed roughly by two men, almost knocking them down.

"Molly! *Molly!*"

If she heard, she didn't turn round.

Michael cursed his wife's independence, though that was one of her most attractive features. He pushed again, but found himself blocked by a woman with two small children. The boy and girl clung to her legs like leeches.

"Mr. Graham."

Glancing behind him, Michael discovered a petite woman trailed him. Not only was she following him, but she had a double-fisted death grip on his leather jacket.

"Sorry." She didn't look apologetic in the least. "But I'm not letting go as long as you're headed out of here. I simply will not allow myself to be trampled."

"Joyce Abernathy." Michael vaguely remembered her name from the introductions.

"You can call me Joyce, if you'd like."

Brilliant. Michael faced the crowded theater again. People had already choked the aisles into gridlock.

"Or if that's too familiar, you can call me Miss Abernathy."

Ignoring the woman for the moment, Michael looked around the room. A dim exit sign hung over a door at the side of the large screen. He sidestepped the mother and her two offspring and headed toward the stage. A throng of people already congregated there, and he pushed through the cloud of perfume, cologne and stale tobacco smoke.

"Where are we going?" Amazingly, Miss Abernathy held on and kept up despite the mismatch between his long legs and her short ones.

"Out."

"Which way is the murder?"

"How should I know?" Michael wanted to find Molly. He shoved the exit door open and it banged against the wall of the building. As he stepped into the cool night, he could smell the salt of the nearby sea as well as fish coming up from the harbor.

"Do you get many murders here? You seem quite calm about this."

"Hardly. If this is a murder, it's the first one that's happened in Blackpool since I've been here." Michael sprinted down the alley behind the theater.

"This must be exciting for you. I know I'm excited."

You're a strange little woman, Miss Abernathy.

"SHE'S OVER HERE."

No more than a step behind Paddington, Molly had to resist passing him. She peered around his burly frame and saw the woman's body crumpled up in the shadows at the edge of the sidewalk near the theater.

Rachel Donner, the woman who'd cried out for help, stood nearby. Molly recognized her now. She was one of the seven survivors. In her seventies, Rachel was slightly plump and short. Age had marked her beauty, and pain and fear now marked it even more. Her hand played at the silver rose pendant hanging from a necklace at her throat. She stood nearly ten feet from the body, her arms wrapped around herself. "There." She grimaced. "Abigail's there. Iris and I were talking. Abigail had stepped away for a cig. She knows I can't handle the smoke with my asthma. The shot came out of nowhere. Someone just shot her."

Although Molly had never seen a dead person outside of a funeral home or church, she was familiar with death through pets. She felt guilty about the comparison almost the moment she made it, but there it was. The woman had a stillness about her that couldn't be mistaken for sleep.

She lay on one side, her gray hair spread loose across the pavement. Surprise and fear had widened her eyes before death. Her lean face showed seventy plus years of a hard life, and her translucent skin was pulled tight over sharp bones. Sea air and the work of a fisherman's wife had roughened her skin and hands.

Paddington pulled a small notebook from inside his coat. He wrote briefly with an ink pen, then retrieved his walkie-talkie from his coat pocket. "Abigail Whiteshire. Run that name for me. Quickly." He spelled it. "Get me an address and phone number." After he tucked the walkie-talkie back into his pocket, he turned his attention to Molly again. "Do you happen to know where the other survivors are?"

Molly shook her head. Then she realized what Paddington was really saying, what made him ask the question— Abigail Whiteshire was one of the survivors, too. A cold chill stole down her back. *Iris. Iris is one of them. God.*

She clenched her fist and made herself remain calm, but she searched the gathering crowd for Michael.

"Maybe we should find out where they are," he said.

"MOLLY." MICHAEL'S HEART calmed a little when he saw that she was all right.

"I'm fine." A short distance away, she stood beside the body of a prone woman. Uniformed police officers surrounded the area.

"Keep those people back." Paddington gestured angrily. "I'll not have them trampling my crime scene."

Immediately two young policemen surged forward and intercepted Michael, an outthrust arm catching him in the chest.

"I'm going to have to ask you to stay there." The policeman was one of Paddington's veterans, grizzled and solid as a fire plug. Before Michael could even shift, the man's fist gripped the fabric of his coat. "Please, sir. Your cooperation would be for the best."

Reluctantly, Michael held his distance.

Joyce Abernathy released her own hold on Michael's coat and sprinted around him. She'd almost gotten past the policemen when the younger one reached out and grabbed her.

"No! No, miss! You can't go over there!"

"Let me go!" Joyce fought against the policeman, but he was twice as big as she was. "Where is Simon?" She strained to see past her captor's shoulder.

Puzzled, Michael tried to remember where Simon Wineguard had gone. The man had disappeared almost as quickly as Molly had.

"Bloody cow! She poked me in the eye!" The young policeman clapped a hand to his face.

The older officer stepped away from Michael, captured

one of Joyce's hands almost effortlessly and snapped hand-cuffs on her. A second later, he pulled the other wrist in and secured it, as well.

"Settle down, miss." His voice was rough and used to giving commands.

"I need to find Simon."

People surged forward as the numbers in the alley increased.

"Is she dead?" A woman only a short distance away from Michael stopped and raised a hand to her mouth. "Oh, my God. Is she dead?"

"Please stay back." The young officer tried to assert his authority while holding a hand to his wounded eye.

"Stay back! Stay back or I'll run the lot of you in!" The older policeman's voice thundered over the crowd and temporarily quieted them.

"Of course she's dead. A lot of people have been killed in this alley."

Everyone's attention swung to a young man with a shaved head and bristling black beard. Neon light from the theater glinted off the gold hoops dangling from his ears. He wore a leather jacket over a long-sleeved shirt and a loose pair of black jeans. The man looked a little more healthy than emaciated, but only a little. His dark eyes gleamed like black fire and he spoke in a rolling, well-modulated voice.

"Don't you remember the stories about Big Nick Berry-hill and how this alley's cursed?" The young man wheeled on the crowd and those nearest him stepped back immediately. He raised his hands to call even more attention to himself. "In 1683, Big Nick Berryhill, captain of the pirate ship *Bloody Breath*—called that because he was fond of telling victims they'd taken their last bloody breath—slew three of his henchmen in this very alley."

Whispers rose among the throng and people drew even farther back.

Michael recognized Liam McKenna then. McKenna was a fairly new arrival to Blackpool, as well, but he'd immersed himself in the town's culture. He and his sister Holly owned and operated Other Syde Haunted Tours, a local tourist attraction that focused on supposedly "haunted" areas of Blackpool.

"Big Nick killed those men without warning." Liam paced the area in front of the crowd like a natural-born showman. "Slit the throats of all three of 'em. Clean as a whistle, he did." He mimed cutting his throat to get his point across better. "Left 'em here in the alley for the rats to feed on."

Mothers pulled their children back, but the kids looked mesmerized by the tale.

Although Michael didn't know Liam McKenna or his sister well, stories circulated about the two of them having criminal pasts. So far they'd done nothing wrong in town.

"Them three men was spying on Big Nick." Liam's voice turned into a conspiratorial rasp. "They were after his treasure. And Big Nick knew it." He flung an arm to encompass the alley. "But as they lay dying, they put a curse on Big Nick Berryhill and everyone in Blackpool that trod through this lane."

"What kind of curse?" The mother of the boy who spoke cuffed him and he yelped.

"Don't encourage that loon," she warned.

"'Loon,' am I?" Liam drew himself up. Dark anger coiled within him and showed in the too-tight smile on his narrow face. "You live in a town of ghosts, of macabre murders, and you say that I am a loon, madam? I'd bet my eyes that the curse those pirates placed on Blackpool is responsible for that poor woman's death."

Muttered curses of another kind filled the alley, but no one spoke them too loudly. A cold breeze from the bay blew over Michael and he turned up the collar of his jacket as the back of his neck prickled.

"Big Nick Berryhill went down with his ship soon after they left Blackpool that murderous night." Liam told his tale with gusto, obviously enjoying the attention.

The older policeman handed off Miss Joyce Abernathy to the younger officer. The woman seemed more calm now, but she still searched the crowd.

"You'll want to be moving along." The older policeman walked toward Liam.

"And if I don't wish to move along?" Liam stood defiantly.

"Then I'm gonna arrest you for disturbing the peace." The officer reached for his truncheon.

Grinning, Liam turned back to his audience. "If any of you want to know more about the ghosts of Blackpool, come see me." He brought business cards out of his jacket pocket and threw them over the crowd like confetti. "I'm Liam McKenna, host of Other Syde Tours. Ghosts are my business." He stepped away just ahead of the policeman reaching for him and melted into the ranks of the crowd.

Michael's iPhone buzzed in his pocket. He thought about ignoring it, then noticed that Molly held hers in her hand with a plea in her eyes. He fished out the phone and glanced at it.

Find Iris. She was with Abigail.

CHAPTER FOUR

MICHAEL LOOKED AT MOLLY and quickly touched his fingertips to his lips. He waved. She nodded but didn't wave in return. Casually as he could, Michael turned and headed back through the mass of people.

Iris Dunstead was their housekeeper. She was also one of the seven survivors Molly had shown on the theater screen along with Abigail Whiteshire—the woman he'd just seen dead on the alley's pavement.

That doesn't mean she's in danger. Michael tried to console himself with that thought as he lifted his phone and brought up his contact list. But he couldn't forget the image of the body in the alley.

And Iris was supposed to be with her. He shivered slightly, and it wasn't the chill this time. He and Molly were quite taken with Iris. She reminded him of a particularly dotty great-aunt he'd had.

The phone rang once and Irwin picked up.

"Good evening, sir."

"There's been a problem."

"The dead woman in the alley. Yes, sir. I'm aware of it."

"I guess bad news travels quickly." Michael turned and walked to the front of the theater. The crowd had thinned but bicycles filled the area.

"Actually, Miss Dunstead told me, sir."

"Miss Dunstead? You've seen her?"

"She's with me now, sir."

In disbelief, Michael looked up the street and saw Irwin standing outside the limousine. The light from the phone illuminated one side of his calm face. Michael suspected that the world could spin off its axis and not draw a raised eyebrow from the German caretaker. He was as taciturn and unflappable as Batman's Alfred.

"She does know that the police—in particular, Inspector Paddington—will want to speak with her," Michael said.

"I'm not certain what she knows at this point, sir. But Miss Dunstead has assured me we have an engagement of some import to tend to. In fact, she was in the process of calling you when you called me."

"What?"

"Perhaps it would be better if you were to take the matter up with her, sir."

"I will." Michael slid the phone into his jacket pocket as he reached the limo. He'd tell Molly he'd found Iris once he'd talked to her.

Irwin opened the rear door as if nothing were amiss.

Miss Iris Dunstead, in her seventies, was lean and fit. She wore a plum-colored evening dress that set off her white corsage, short white hair and white gloves, giving her a regal appearance. She even wore makeup. Michael could have counted the number of times that had happened on the fingers of one hand.

"Oh, please, Michael." Iris shook her head slightly. "Don't stand out there with your mouth open. You'll swallow a fly or some other dreadful insect." She scooted over and patted the seat beside her. "Please hurry. If we're in luck, we're going to catch the murderers."

MOLLY STARED AT THE iPhone in her hand and willed it to flash on with a text message. She worked hard not to stare at Abigail Whiteshire's body, but the task was impossible. She couldn't help wondering how the woman had been killed and if she was somehow responsible.

Of course you're somewhat responsible. You set up the event this evening. You let yourself get caught up in the history of the robbery. Abigail Whiteshire wouldn't have been here if you hadn't arranged everything.

A portly man carrying a black bag called to Paddington from the crowd.

The inspector yanked his glare from Molly and peered at the new arrival. Then he waved. "Dr. Littleton. Good of you to join us."

Littleton held up his bag. "I thought perhaps you'd need me."

"I do."

The police officers widened the line enough to let Littleton through. The doctor was in his fifties with a clean-shaven face and a thin mustache. Horn-rimmed glasses gave him a professorial appearance. He wore a black suit and a long coat.

As he passed Molly, Dr. Littleton touched his hat in greeting. "Evening, Mrs. Graham. I must say, it was an excellent party until…this."

"Thank you."

Littleton knelt down beside the victim. In addition to his duties as a physician, he also held the post of coroner. Usually the crime scenes he worked were mishaps and pub brawls that had ended lethally.

He let go of the dead woman's arm. The limb flopped lifelessly to the ground. He pressed his fingers against her neck. "She appears to have been shot with a pistol at close range, judging from the powder burns. I'd say death was instant. I'll know more later."

Paddington nodded. "That'll do for now, Doctor. Is her handbag under her body?"

Littleton turned his attention back to the dead woman. "Give me a hand, would you?" Together, he and Paddington rolled the lifeless body up and peered under it. "No handbag here."

"What about a pocketbook?"

The doctor searched the dead woman's clothing, then leaned back in surprise. "There doesn't seem to be one."

"I've never met a woman who didn't travel with a handbag or pocketbook." Paddington searched the ground, flicking the torch around carefully. "That means hers has to be here somewhere."

Molly stepped back and scanned the vicinity, as well. Her iPhone buzzed for attention.

Found Iris.

She tapped the keys like lightning. Where?

She was with Irwin.

WHAT ARE YOU doing?

Michael stared at the text on his phone and wondered that exact same thing. If he had any sense, he'd—

"Contact Paddington?" Iris lifted her left eyebrow sarcastically. "That's what you're thinking, isn't it?"

Guilt crashed over Michael as he met the older woman's

gaze. He hadn't been able to hide anything from his great-aunt, either. He sighed. Then his iPhone vibrated again.

Michael?

Irwin piloted the limo through the darkened streets at well past the posted speed limits.

"Paddington would seem like the logical course of action." Michael tapped a quick message to Molly.

Patience, love.

Iris blew a raspberry and shook her head. "You saw how mired he is there at the back of the theater. By the time he could get free, the men we're after will be long gone. It's a good thing I told Rachel to go home and wait there for the police to get to her. Her nerves wouldn't have been able to take this."

"Men?" Michael's stomach turned cold and felt like it had been filled with broken glass.

"Yes. Two of them. One shot that poor woman while the other drove a motorbike to make their getaway." Iris smoothed her coat. "I refuse to let that happen. Bad enough I saw them murder her."

"Getaway?" Michael knew Iris loved murder mysteries, though she was actually a writer of historical novels. She and Molly shared favorite authors and chatted about books they'd read.

"As I said, two men drove up on a motorbike. One got off and shot Abigail to death. He searched her and took her handbag. By that time, Rachel and I were shouting at them. Rachel ran for help while I watched helpless, as the men got back on their motorbike and drove away. Would you call it something other than a getaway?"

"No." Michael looked through the front window. Irwin drove smoothly. "You saw them do this?"

"Yes."

"Why did they attack her?"

"I don't know. Rachel and I were out in the alley before Abigail. Maybe they left us alone because there were two of us, but I think they were after Abigail."

"Why?"

"While that one searched her, he took something from his pocket—a phone, perhaps. He looked at Abigail again, snatched the handbag and they were gone in seconds."

Immediately, Michael's mind spun, bouncing off the various angles that his imagination supplied him with. "What were you doing out in the alley?"

An uncomfortable expression crossed Iris's face. "To be quite frank, I found myself feeling a bit under the weather. Rachel walked me out to get some air."

"She was nervous, sir." Irwin looked back in the rearview mirror. "Tonight's introduction at the event didn't agree with her."

"Was that why Abigail was out there?"

"She was having a cig," Iris said.

"Okay." The iPhone buzzed in Michael's hands again, but he ignored it when he saw it was Molly wanting an update. "So they were after her handbag?"

"I don't know. It all happened so fast."

Michael took a breath and let it out. "Where are we going?"

"To Abigail's house."

"Why would the murderers go there?"

"Because they didn't get what they were looking for."

"How do you know that?"

"Because I heard one of them say 'It's not here!'" Iris

shrugged. "I'm thinking that's why they took her purse—to get her keys."

Michael considered what they were facing and sat back in the seat. His mouth was dry and his tongue felt thick. He didn't know if he hoped Irwin arrived in time or not.

CHAPTER FIVE

IRWIN PULLED THE LIMOUSINE to a halt beside the curb. The luxury car almost filled the street and drew the attention of a few neighbors.

Before Michael realized what Iris was doing, she had opened the door and slid out.

"Iris." Michael scrambled after her but was hard pressed to catch up. The years hadn't seemed to slow the housekeeper and she was thin as a greyhound.

"Don't forget to take pictures, Michael." Iris never turned around as she headed straight for a three-story building. "I'm sure the inspector would prefer a photograph of the murderers instead of our descriptions."

Frustrated but recognizing she had a point, Michael hurried back to the car and reached inside for his computer bag. By the time he'd grabbed the digital camera from one of the pockets—he never traveled without a camera—Iris was already across the street. He silently cursed, but his heart was pounding fiercely and he knew he was equally caught up in the anticipation of the chase. He thrived on competition and relished physical exertion.

But *murderers!*

At the back of the limousine, Irwin opened the trunk and took out a tire iron. Michael stared at the crooked metal rod.

"I hope you don't think that's going to be necessary."

Irwin grimaced. "I rather hope not, Mr. Graham. But I

don't like taking chances considering the situation we're presently in." He tried a smile but it didn't quite come off. "Personally, I'd prefer a handgun. Something chambered in large caliber and possessing a huge magazine."

Not for the first time, Michael wondered about Irwin's past. The man hadn't always been a caretaker, but he'd never bothered to fill in all the blank spots on his resume. He knew the oddest things.

Michael sprinted after Iris and caught up with her on the second-floor landing. "Do you know which flat Abigail lived in?"

"Number three." Iris kept her hand on the banister as she pulled herself along. "At the corner."

Michael stepped in front of her. "Would you please wait here with Irwin?"

Iris hesitated, then she nodded in obvious irritation. "Rather than have you worrying about me and be distracted, I'll agree to that. For the moment." She stared into his eyes. "If you should need help—"

"You'll know." Michael walked along the narrow landing toward the flat at the end.

"Be careful."

He wanted to tell her that being careful involved staying in the limousine. Instead, he concentrated on the flat ahead of him and tried not to think of all the private investigator movies he'd watched where the hero got whacked on the head for his troubles.

When he found the door slightly ajar, Michael hoped it meant they were too late. Unless Abigail Whiteshire hadn't closed her door well on her way out.

From the corner of his eye, he saw Iris straining to watch him. Irwin stood silently beside her, the tire iron hanging from his hand.

Michael took shelter beside the door and hoped that

the men they'd come after had somehow lost their guns. Knives would be bad enough, but it was possible to outrun a knife. He made himself breathe out because he was hyperventilating.

Then he used his elbow to open the unlocked door.

Nothing stirred inside.

"Whatever are you doing?"

The voice came from up above and Michael almost bolted when he heard it. He tracked the question to an elderly woman standing on the landing, peering down at him.

"Call the coppers." Michael shook his head at his choice of words. The term had come too easily. *Too many crime movies.*

The woman disappeared, presumably to make that very call.

After he fished his iPhone from his pocket, he switched on the flashlight app. The beam from the rectangular screen wasn't strong, but it illuminated the dark interior of the flat. Feeling fearful, he walked inside.

Overturned furniture lay scattered across the carpeted floor. Michael assumed that Abigail Whiteshire was normally much neater, but hardly anything looked organized now. The living room was sectioned off into a dining room, as well, and a closet door stood open, coats and clothing spilling onto the floor.

Whoever had broken into the house had obviously been in a hurry.

"Michael?"

"I'm all right, Iris." Michael turned and shined the phone around the room. Sudden movement to his right sent him into a panic. He dodged to one side and managed to topple a vase of flowers, which smashed against the floor.

"Michael!"

A soot-gray cat on the window ledge hissed and spat. Its eyes lit up as orange as cigarette coals in the phone's light. Fear rippled its muscles and it arched its back.

Feeling foolish and inept, Michael regained his balance. "It was nothing. I tripped. Abigail had a cat."

"I should have mentioned the cat. He's very territorial. His name is Ambrose."

Michael gave the cat a wide berth as it followed him with its malevolent gaze. He started to relax despite the shambles of the flat.

If the men who had killed Abigail Whiteshire and broken into her home were still about, surely they would have confronted him by now.

And if they had, you might be dead. It wasn't a pleasant thought and he tried to dismiss it, but it hovered there at the back of his mind.

"Have they already gone, then?"

Glancing over his shoulder, Michael spotted Iris in the doorway. "Couldn't wait?"

"I didn't see the need to. Other than the vase breaking, there were no other sounds. Except your breathing. Besides, I knew that Ambrose would be awfully upset." Iris went to the cat and reached for it.

With obvious reluctance, the feline allowed Iris to pick it up. After a moment, though, the cat nestled into her embrace.

"I gather we're alone, sir?" Irwin stood in the door with the tire iron in hand.

"For the moment, I suppose. I'm sure the neighbor upstairs has called the police by now." Michael wondered just what had just happened here. He looked at Iris. "Any idea what they could have been after?"

"No." Iris glanced around her as she stroked the cat. "But it's easy enough to see they were after something."

Out in the street, tires screeched on pavement. Then doors opened with metallic pops.

"The police have arrived." Irwin remained as solemn as ever.

"Perhaps it would be better if we met them outside." Michael led the way.

Two uniformed officers pounded up the stairs as Michael stepped onto the landing. They froze and drew truncheons.

"It's all right." Michael held his hands up to show they were empty. "I'm not here to hurt anyone. I came to check on Mrs. Whiteshire's home, that's all."

Quietly, the policemen started up the steps again.

"What's going on, mate?" The older man shined a light in Michael's eyes.

"Came here to check on the flat, like I said. Found it already broken into."

"That right?" The policeman's tone indicated that he wasn't all that trusting.

"That's right." Michael sighed; he wasn't going to get back to his game design and thoughts of mermaids any time soon.

MOLLY SAT IN THE COLD ROOM and tried to summon warm thoughts. Instead, all she could think about was Abigail Whiteshire and how small the dead woman had looked in the alley.

The Blackpool Police Department was currently head-quartered in an old converted Victorian house only a few streets back from the marina. Amid the hum of computers and ringing telephones, the clangor of rigging slapping against boat and ship masts out in the harbor could be heard, pulling the station's atmosphere back to the nineteenth century. The small rooms and bay windows furthered the illusion.

The room Molly sat in was bereft of creature comforts. Only a small table bolted to the floor and four folding chairs around it provided any kind of furnishing. Bleak and empty, the walls seemed to close in on her as she sat there awaiting Paddington's convenience.

Molly's eyes burned from fatigue. Before tonight, she'd put in a lot of long hours preparing for the event at the theater, and paving the way in the community for the documentary crew. But now everything was up in the air. The realization soured her mood.

The door opened and Paddington walked through carrying a folder under one arm and two cups of coffee.

Sitting up straighter, Molly watched the inspector take a seat across from her. The chair legs screeched on the floor as he drew in closer to the table.

"Coffee?" Paddington held up a disposable cup.

"Please." Molly accepted the proffered drink. "Thank you." Her hands wrapped around it and gratefully absorbed the warmth.

"You're welcome. Usually I drink tea, but this promises to be a late night." Paddington flipped open the folder and pulled out his notebook. "We picked up your husband. Apparently he got it into his head that he might intercept Abigail Whiteshire's murderers at her flat. Do you know why he might think that?" He fixed her with his piercing gaze.

"Iris—our housekeeper—and another woman, Rachel Donner, witnessed the murder. Iris—"

Paddington held up a big, rough hand. "Please, Mrs. Graham, spare me. Your husband evidently arrived at the address only minutes after the murderers ransacked Mrs. Whiteshire's home and departed. Thankfully they didn't hang about to crack his skull for his trouble. He could have just as easily been in the hospital for his foolishness instead of outside in the waiting room. What he should have done was call the police."

"I agree. But apparently Iris didn't leave Michael much choice. She can be quite…forceful." Molly didn't actually agree with Paddington, though if Michael had gotten hurt she might have felt differently.

Paddington seemed surprised by her answer. He sipped his coffee to cover his reaction. "We also found Mr. Wineguard."

"He's well?"

"He is. Apparently he thought he might be hurt next. Is there any reason for him to believe that?"

"Simon tends to be high-strung and perhaps a trifle paranoid. Comes from a creative mind, I guess."

"Or a guilty one."

"Why would Simon harm Abigail Whiteshire?"

Lacing his thick fingers on the table, Paddington shrugged. "Perhaps you can tell me."

"Simon met the woman once."

"People have been known to kill individuals they've never met, Mrs. Graham. And Mr. Wineguard wasn't sitting in the audience where he was supposed to be. Maybe he was coordinating the attack with two of his cronies."

Molly didn't have an answer for that. She hadn't known where Simon was before the introduction. Not for the first time, suspicions slithered through her mind, though she could find no basis for them.

"So you can't imagine a motive for Wineguard to murder Abigail Whiteshire?"

Molly forced herself to remain calm. "Inspector, let's make one thing perfectly clear—if I'd thought anyone was in danger tonight because of this event, I would have canceled it."

Paddington leaned back in his chair and scratched his head tiredly. "I'm sure it was also just fortuitous that Liam McKenna happened to be at the theater tonight to start tongues wagging with his tales of vengeful pirate ghosts? That will certainly create a lot of gossip."

More than the murder? Drawing a breath, Molly looked at Paddington. "The whole evening tonight was designed to draw most—if not all—of Blackpool into the area. That was why we had a free movie and catering. Am I really supposed to be surprised that Liam McKenna was there hoping to hawk his ghost tours?"

The inspector's eyes remained dead. "I told you from the beginning that this whole affair was a bad idea."

"You can't prove that Abigail Whiteshire's murder was connected to the documentary."

"Do I need proof, Mrs. Graham? This...*event*...is the only unusual thing that's going on at present. The festival coming up will be a pain in the posterior, but that's something we here in Blackpool have come to accept as a necessary evil." He waved a hand. "This bit with the train robbery, though, isn't."

"The train robbery occurred over seventy years ago." Molly forced her voice to remain even. "It seems very unlikely Mrs. Whiteshire was murdered because of that."

Paddington rubbed his jaw. "And yet it would be to Mr. Wineguard's considerable benefit to have one of these seven *survivors* murdered. I suspect that the attention that would generate would be nothing but good news for him."

That Paddington could even believe people on the documentary crew would have committed the murder for mere publicity sickened Molly.

"Fred Purnell is beside himself because one of the BBC

news channels is sending a group of reporters out to Blackpool to cover the investigation," Paddington continued. "He's certain they're going to scoop him on a murder played out in his own backyard." He scowled. "I don't have to tell you that I'm not overly sympathetic to his concerns."

Molly's mind spun. She would have to address the outside media, as well. And their presence in Blackpool was definitely going to throw off the documentary's shooting schedule.

"So now I have to deal with out-of-town reporters set on turning a molehill into a mountain." Paddington shook his head irritably. "If I could, I'd lock down the whole lot of them as soon as they step into town."

"That attitude certainly won't win you any friends."

"Frankly, Mrs. Graham, I have enough friends. And now I have more than enough murders to investigate."

Molly didn't have a response to that, so she decided to keep quiet.

"For the time being, I'm going to let you go." Paddington closed the file.

"I haven't done anything wrong. You have no right to hold me."

Paddington grinned coldly. "Trust me. If I'd wanted you around here longer, it would have happened. I could have arrested your husband, your housekeeper and your caretaker for trespassing and interfering with a police investigation—just for starters. I'm choosing not to do that as an exercise in good judgment. I'm hoping for reciprocity from you and the documentary crew. I don't want you trying to mix this into your little fable."

"Of course not." *Unless it* does *tie into the story.* Molly considered the possibility, but it seemed far too weak at this point. Testing the waters, she stood and picked up her coffee.

Paddington made no move to stop her.

"What about the other survivors?" Molly felt guilty that she'd been primarily concerned about Iris. She'd gotten to know the other six people somewhat over the last few weeks.

"You already know about Mrs. Dunstead and Rachel Donner." The inspector slid his small notebook back into his jacket pocket. "The other four are safe, as well."

Some of Molly's tension went away. "Good. I'm glad."

"Is there any reason I should worry about the rest of them?"

"Not to my knowledge."

"I'll keep an eye on them anyway. For a while." Paddington stood. "If I have any more questions, Mrs. Graham, I'll be in touch."

"Of course." Molly walked through the door at his invitation, but her mind swam with her own questions.

CHAPTER SIX

MICHAEL SAT WITH IRWIN and Iris out in the small waiting area of the police station. Rachel Donner had been picked up and brought in to give her statement. She was currently in an interview room. A dozen people, most of them Simon Wineguard's film crew, sprawled tiredly in uncomfortable chairs. All of them looked as though they'd just been through combat.

Wineguard sat nearest the door of the room. Joyce Abernathy, oddly, was sitting as far from him as possible. Simon glanced up when Molly walked in and smiled without any enthusiasm. "We're off to a rather auspicious beginning, my dear. Don't you agree?"

Molly nodded. "Is there anything I can do?"

"Not that I know of." Wineguard flicked his gaze to Paddington. "I assume the inspector has some questions he'd like answered. Not that I have many of the answers, I'm afraid." Then he smiled. "But on the bright side, I hear that the BBC has a news team en route."

Towering over the director, Paddington scowled.

"So I heard." Molly took out her iPhone and started composing a list. "I'll see what I can do to help with that."

"Whatever you do, be a dear and don't make them go away. We couldn't pay for this kind of publicity."

Molly acknowledged that fact, and she felt guilty that both of them were already looking for the silver lining in Abigail Whiteshire's murder.

"You go along, my dear." Wineguard shooed her away with a hand. "I'll keep the inspector company tonight. We'll meet tomorrow—I'll call you—and we'll timeline our operations given our new circumstances."

Molly nodded and left, collecting Michael, Irwin and Iris from the waiting room. As they all climbed into the car, she slid her hand gratefully into Michael's and found his flesh warm and reassuring. She had to get home where she could think and plan.

"ARE YOU ALL RIGHT?"

Molly glanced up from the hastily constructed notes on her iPhone and saw Michael watching her. Worry darkened his eyes. "I'm fine." She even smiled a little for him.

They sat in the back of the limousine on the ride to their manor house, Irwin and Iris in the front. They lived just outside of Blackpool proper and usually enjoyed the drive. Forest filled the roadside to the west and the bay lay sparkling to the east. Glower Lighthouse glowed to the north as it stood guard over the treacherous waters filled with broken rock.

"Were you friends with…" Michael hesitated, but Molly knew what he was trying to ask.

"Abigail Whiteshire?"

Michael nodded. "Sorry, love. I had to ask."

"Iris knew her more than I did. She introduced us after she found out what I was working on. She and Abigail were childhood friends. As they got older, they grew apart. Iris didn't stay around Blackpool like Abigail did."

That had been the first inkling Molly had gotten that their housekeeper had had a life outside of the town. Iris had never before offered such information.

"Do you think her death had anything to do with the documentary?" Michael gazed at her with concern.

Molly smiled at him reassuringly. He wasn't a worrier by nature. That was one of the things she loved about him. Michael took everything in stride. But he was innately curious; he didn't like situations he couldn't fathom, and he didn't like puzzles he couldn't solve. He was also protective of her. She loved that about him, as well.

"No." Molly leaned her head against his shoulder and felt the solid weight of him. "Nothing at all. This was just a sad thing. Probably a robbery gone badly wrong."

"Perhaps. But why go to her house after they killed her?"

"Iris said they didn't find whatever they were looking for. Maybe she didn't have any money on her and they thought they could find some at her home. If they took her handbag and the keys were inside, they likely thought they had more time to steal whatever might be there."

"They seemed to make that decision awfully quickly."

Molly looked at him and lifted an inquiring eyebrow. "What are you saying?"

"These blokes were ruthless, determined and selective. Like Iris, I don't think Abigail Whiteshire was a victim of casual misfortune."

"You mean they specifically targeted her?" The thought chilled Molly.

Michael nodded. "Yes. As you said, they were looking for something, love. And Abigail Whiteshire didn't have much more than that tabby Iris is doting on, so why go to her house?"

"You think she had something they wanted."

"I do. Unfortunately, I don't know what it was."

"Something small enough to carry on her person."

"And something they thought she'd have with her tonight. Otherwise they'd have burgled her flat first."

"The inspector seems determined to blame the documentary crew, and Simon Wineguard in particular."

"Any idea where he was tonight?"

Molly slapped her husband's broad chest. "Not you, too. Simon wouldn't hurt a fly."

"Maybe you should be open to a little more cynicism."

"Thanks, but no. One cynic in the family is enough."

"I thought I was more often accused of being the optimist."

Despite everything that had happened, Molly smiled. She felt safe in Michael's arms. "You're usually the optimist. However, I've seen you be quite cynical on occasion. If circumstances warrant."

"These do."

"Paddington may have the men responsible for the murder locked up by morning." Molly hoped that would be the case, but she honestly doubted it. The particulars surrounding Abigail Whiteshire's murder were too strange to believe an easy solution could be found.

"There's a cheery thought. Unless he locks up Simon Wineguard. Or someone else from the documentary crew." Michael paused, looking amused. "Did I tell you that Miss Abernathy is a strange little bird?"

"I already knew that, but that woman is indestructible. She worked me to death the one time I agreed to do Pilates with her. She was like Arnold Schwarzenegger in *The Terminator*." Molly closed her eyes and concentrated on enjoying the rest of the trip home. She willed her mind to relax and stop lunging into dark thoughts, but that didn't happen.

Her iPhone rang at the same time as Michael's. In the driver's seat, Irwin pulled his cell phone from his jacket, as well.

Molly tapped the screen with practiced ease, answering the call before Michael could pick up. "Hello?"

"Mrs. Graham, this is Holdover Security." The voice was polite and male, totally professional and calm. "We just recorded a break-in at your house and wanted to make sure you and your family were all right."

MICHAEL FORCED HIMSELF to sit quietly in the seat beside Molly as she called the Blackpool Police Department. From the exchange, he gathered that DCI Paddington wasn't gracious about being directed from his homicide investigation. He became even less gracious when Molly told him about the security company alert. After a brief conversation, heated at the inspector's end, Molly punched off the connection.

"He wants us to stay away from the house." Molly put her phone back inside her purse.

"Of course he does. But it's not his bloody house, is it? By the time he gets a patrol car out here, we could have lost all our things." Michael hated the helplessness that coursed through him.

"They're just things, Michael." Molly stroked his temple. "Whatever is lost, we can replace."

For her sake, he tried to be calm. If they were indeed robbed, he would feel more violated than she did. Molly didn't put a lot of value in material possessions. She'd grown up with them. But he had worked for everything he had, and he'd started out with precious little in life.

"I know, love." Michael captured her hand and kissed her palm. But silently he urged Irwin to greater speed as they careened down the two-lane highway.

Just before he reached the gated entrance to Thorne-Shower Mansion, Irwin doused the limousine's lights and glided to a halt. The decision surprised Michael. He'd only just considered switching off the lights, but Irwin seemed to have done it instinctively.

"Sir, if I may." The caretaker spoke without turning around. He also reached up and turned off the interior lights before they came on.

"You may." Michael opened the door and started to get out.

"I'd suggest the ladies stay with the car. They'll be safer here."

"Maybe the ladies don't want to be left behind." Molly opened the door on her side. Iris obviously agreed, as she was out of the car just as quickly.

"As you wish, Mrs. Graham." Quietly, Irwin eased from his seat. He had the tire iron in hand once more.

"Molly." Michael kept his voice soft.

Her eyes flashed as she glanced at him. "No. If you're going, I'm going. Otherwise we can wait together."

Michael sighed unhappily. Waiting wasn't something he was good at. Of course, he wasn't crazy about the idea of catching burglars in the act, either.

"All right."

Iris trailed after them.

At the gate, Irwin pulled a large key ring from his coat, sorted through the collection, made a selection and inserted it into the small wrought-iron gate beside the larger one. They passed through without speaking.

When Michael had first seen Thorne-Shower Mansion, he'd almost walked away from it. The three-story home was close to two centuries old and stood like a Victorian monolith among a wilderness of trees. The "road," though it could hardly be called that, that led from the rusty gates to the house had been overgrown with grass.

The mansion hadn't been entirely deserted. Iris Dunstead had lived there as housekeeper, and one of the conditions of sale had been for her to continue living there. Michael still didn't know what arrangements had been made to assure that, but the stipulation was nonnegotiable. And, in the end, it had proven moot because the older woman and Molly had gotten along brilliantly.

Now, after extensive repairs and upgrades to the interior, Michael loved the house. The location, only minutes from the bay and less than half an hour from Blackpool, was ideal.

Michael peered through the darkness. He'd grown up outside London, but he'd been a metropolitan dweller most of his life. Forests were all well and proper during the daylight hours, but he didn't care for them at night. Too many things tended to be lurking within the darkness and shadows.

Only a few minutes later, they stood outside the main house. Security lights lit the mansion. Michael watched the windows, trying in vain to discern movement.

"Seems bloody stupid to be standing outside, afraid to go into your own house." He snorted angrily.

"Mr. Graham, I believe it would be as stupid to blindly charge in while not knowing what awaits us." In the darkest shadows, Irwin was almost invisible.

For a moment the idea that the man might not even be flesh-and-blood crossed Michael's mind. He dismissed it and silently chuckled at himself. *You are spooked, mate. Lighten up.*

"Actually…we can see what's going on in the house without going in." Michael took his iPhone from his pocket and brought up the Internet. After a couple entries, he logged on to the Holdover Security site. "I can access the security cameras inside the house." When he had decided on a security system, he'd put in the best one money could buy. Molly had teased him about his love of technology, but the system wasn't much more expensive with the video access upgrade.

Molly leaned in over his shoulder. "I didn't know you could do that."

"I showed you. Your phone can do the same thing. Obviously you weren't listening that day."

"I always listen. It's just that some of the things that you find so fascinating about technology…aren't. At least not to me."

"So kind of you to mention that." Michael flipped through the menu and checked the rooms. The different camera views only took a few seconds to load. The ability to examine every room made him feel more in control of everything that was going on.

"Doesn't appear to be anyone inside." The cold night air fogged Molly's breath as she spoke, but the vapor vanished almost as soon as her words escaped her lips.

Michael peered at the road that wove through the landscaped grounds. The trees came to a stop within forty feet of the main house.

The drive circled in front of the manor, then wound out around the garage and the small house where Irwin and Iris lived in separate quarters. Lights were on in those buildings, as well.

Michael glanced to Irwin. "The cars, do you think?"

"They would be the most valuable asset to seize, sir, but they would also be hard to escape with, given the road conditions around Blackpool."

That was true. Blackpool remained somewhat removed from other cities and towns, and the highways and roads definitely lacked hospitality.

"Unless the thieves intended to get them away by boat."

Michael frowned at the caretaker. "It bothers me that you're so quick with that answer."

Irwin permitted himself a sliver of a grin. "One's mind does tend to wander while polishing an auto, sir."

"True." Michael gripped the iPhone and took a breath. "I'm going to assume that whoever was here has already gone. And found a way out. Let's have a look at what they did."

Thankfully, Molly stayed slightly behind him as he and Irwin headed toward the house. Michael's stomach lurched as he crossed the distance to the main door. Surprisingly, it was locked. He reached into his pocket.

"Permit me, sir." Irwin stepped forward with his key ring and quickly unlocked the door. The mechanism clicked hollowly and echoed in the large room beyond.

Cautiously, Michael entered the house.

CHAPTER SEVEN

"So THE INTRUDERS WERE IN the house seven minutes?"

Taking a deep breath to ease his frustration, Michael nodded at the inspector. "We've got some nice footage of a couple blokes in ski masks trashing the house, but not much else."

"I'll need a copy of that."

"Of course." Michael looked past DCI Paddington into Molly's office on the first floor. She occupied a large suite just off the grand ballroom. Normally that office was kept neat as a pin. Iris Dunstead never stepped foot into the place to clean, although she was a frequent guest there. The room was entirely Molly's domain.

Bulletin boards, dry erase boards and computer equipment covered the walls as if placed there according to an architect's design. Color-coded folders, always kept in filing cabinets, now lay strewn across the floor like scattered plumage from an enormous and multihued bird.

Molly's large Victorian desk sat on the other side of the room, its drawers overturned on the Persian rug.

Unbelievably, Molly kept herself under control as Paddington's crime scene team—such as it was—tramped through the office. She stood to one side with her arms crossed and fury in her eyes. Michael was relieved that he wasn't one of the people who had caused the room's destruction.

Paddington carefully stepped through the debris. "Seven minutes, you say."

"They were here at least seven minutes. They tripped one of the interior alarms. I'm not sure when the outer alarm was breached." Michael kept himself detached from the fear that quivered inside him. He couldn't help thinking what might have happened if Molly had been home at the time of the break-in. He wanted to believe the thieves simply would have waited for the house to be empty.

"What?" Paddington paused with his pen above his notebook.

"Whoever broke in set off a security alarm." Michael spoke slowly, working through the possible scenario in his mind. "But they might have been here awhile before they set the alarm off." He focused on Paddington. "In fact, they could have been prowling around my house while you had us cooling our heels at the police station."

Paddington ignored the jibe. "If they got around the security in this house, they weren't just sods off the farm, were they?"

"I suppose not."

"Was anything taken?"

Michael shook his head. "All the computer equipment, the tellys seem to be here. We're going to go through the computers before we use them, of course."

"For?"

"Malware. Little nasty bits of programming that might compromise our security."

"Do you do your banking over the Internet?"

"Of course. But we also do a lot of work online."

"You think that might have been what the thieves were after? Your work?"

Michael let out a slow breath and tried not to show his frustration. "No."

"Why?"

"People good enough to hack the encryption on my computers wouldn't need to be here physically to do it, and I'm too small a target for them."

The inspector looked around the house. "You and the missus seem to have done all right for yourselves."

"We don't keep anything in the house that would tempt the smash-and-grab set."

"You're a computer designer. Video games. Bestselling video games, the way I hear it. And Mrs. Graham is successful, as well."

Michael nodded.

"Maybe someone just assumed you had something to steal."

"That sounds random, but as you said yourself, this was clearly done by people who knew what they were about."

Paddington gazed at him in deliberate speculation. "Then why was your house broken into?"

"I couldn't tell you, Inspector."

"Maybe I can." He nodded toward Molly's office. "Someone was looking for something."

"Inspector—"

"They didn't bother with your office. Or anywhere else in the house that I can see."

Michael didn't argue the point. His office was in the same messy shape it had been when he'd left it. Nothing had been touched, and there was plenty to handle. A lot of expensive computer hardware filled the shelves. Kids would have definitely nicked the video game components.

"Just your wife's office." Paddington made another note. "I find that quite interesting."

"It wasn't just the office, Inspector."

Michael glanced at the uniformed officer who walked up to join them. The woman was tall and thin and looked too young to be a police officer. Her hair was pulled back in a severe ponytail.

"What have you got, Saylor?"

It took Michael a moment to figure out the woman's name was Saylor.

She pointed an index finger over her shoulder. "The maid's—"

"Housekeeper." Iris joined the woman. "Domestic engineer if you want to be snooty. I'm not a maid."

The female officer glanced at Michael.

Michael nodded quickly. "Iris isn't a maid."

Saylor rolled her gaze over to Paddington in a show of polite exasperation. "As it turns out, this woman's living quarters were ransacked, as well."

"YOU DIDN'T REALIZE YOUR HOME had been broken into?"

Still holding the cat, Iris Dunstead leveled a reproachful look at DCI Paddington. During her association with Iris, Molly had seen grown men melt under that gaze. Paddington didn't, but he did wait for Iris to reply.

"This is the first time I've been back since I left with Rachel Donner earlier in the evening. She offered to drive and I went with her. She didn't want to go alone." Iris turned to face the door to her second-floor quarters.

The smaller house had been generously appointed when Molly and Michael bought the mansion, and most of the furniture within these rooms belonged to Iris. Molly had offered all of the wiring and electronic upgrades she and Michael had made to the main house, and Iris had accepted. Still, the lamps remained from an earlier era and an otherworldly quality emanated from the colored glass.

During the time she'd been at the mansion, Molly had been a guest here as frequently as Iris had been at the main house. They had a lot in common, although both kept their personal lives private and were comfortable with that.

Molly had grown curious about Iris, but never enough to pry. Whenever someone Iris had known from years ago talked about her, though, Molly always listened for tidbits of the woman's past. There were still large gaps in her personal history that she didn't know.

"When we got back, we investigated the main house." Iris calmly stroked the cat and it purred audibly in pleasure.

"None of you thought to come back here?" Paddington scanned the mess that started just inside Iris's door and continued throughout the rooms.

"Why would we? The only disturbance we knew about was in Molly's office, and that was bad enough." Iris shook her head. "This...this is reprehensible."

Several of her photo albums had been flung across the floor. Photographs lay abandoned but Molly thought it looked like someone had been through them.

"So why did they only search your and Mrs. Graham's rooms?"

"I'm hardly an expert when it comes to the criminal mind, Inspector."

One of the uniformed crime scene investigators moved slowly through Iris's quarters, taking snapshots with a digital camera. Molly's heart went out to Iris. Having her office torn up was one thing, but Iris *lived* in these rooms. That invasion of privacy cut much deeper.

"Can you tell if anything's missing?"

Iris shook her head. "I'll have to do a proper inventory." Then she focused on the couch and frowned slightly. "There is something missing. I had a box beside the couch. I don't see it anywhere at the moment."

"A box?" Intrigue stamped on his face, Paddington stepped inside the room. "What kind of box?"

"Cardboard. It once held envelopes for the post." Iris followed the inspector and Molly trailed after her.

"What does it hold now?"

"Photographs that Molly and I gathered from different residents of Blackpool. Dozens of them."

Noticing Iris and Molly on his heels for the first time, Paddington sighed, then directed them out of the room again. "Please, ladies."

"It's not like we're going to do any more damage than has already been done." Iris's tone was sharp and Molly put her hand on the older woman's shoulder.

"No, Mrs. Dunstead, you're not," the inspector said. "And I apologize for my behavior. I don't mean to act so callous, but we have to maintain the integrity of the scene."

"And I'm quite sure the Blackpool police force has better things to do than investigate a simple case of breaking and entering," Iris said.

"We do." Paddington's eyes glowed with an inner heat. "But it's fairly clear that this was not a simple forced entry."

Molly was convinced it wasn't, but she didn't want to voice her opinion. That would give it too much strength and resonance, place it too deeply in her and Michael's lives. As well as Iris's and Irwin's. The very thought stripped away precious feelings of safety and security.

"What was so special about those photographs?" Paddington waited patiently. "What had you and Mrs. Graham collected?"

"They were all from around the time of the train robbery."

"Ah." The inspector nodded ponderously. "I thought as much. You'll have to admit that, in light of the murder only a short time ago, this crime takes on a whole other aspect."

WHEN MICHAEL WOKE THE NEXT morning, he rolled over to an empty bed. He glanced at the clock on the nightstand and saw the time was 10:14 a.m. Sleeping till the late hour didn't bother him. Paddington and his police officers hadn't left till shortly after four o'clock.

Groggy, he shoved the blankets back and flinched at the morning's chill. He pulled on a pair of pajama pants, a T-shirt featuring a sword-carrying elf from one of his video games, and stepped into slippers. Then he slapped his arms to invigorate his circulation the way he'd seen his father do. The effort didn't do anything except make his arms sting, and he was slowly coming to realize that even at thirty he was turning into his father. The thought didn't make him comfortable even though he had a good relationship with his dad and respected him.

The bedroom reflected more of Molly's nature than his. She'd filled it with hundred-year-old furniture heavy enough to use as ship's anchors, then frilled the windows and floor with curtains and carpets. The sole concession to Michael and the twenty-first century was the large-screen television mounted on the wall.

He pulled the remote from his side of the bed where it always was, clicked away from the movie he'd been watching, and went to live broadcast. Muting the audio, he flicked through the channels provided by the satellite connection till he found a BBC news station.

He lifted his phone from the nightstand and called Molly. She didn't answer till the fourth ring and he'd just started wondering if she'd left the house when she picked up.

"Good morning." Despite everything that had happened last night, her voice sounded chipper.

Michael smiled. "I've got an empty bed. Very disappointing."

"You looked like you needed your beauty rest."

"I'd rather chance looking like an ogre to spend a quiet morning with you."

"There's no chance of that today, I'm afraid."

"Disheartening."

"I would have wanted nothing more. But there's a lot to do this morning if I'm going to help Simon save the documentary."

A headline on the television caught Michael's eye. He flicked the hearing-impaired function on and scanned the story.

BRUTAL MURDER ROCKS SEASIDE TOWN. BLACKPOOL EVENT INVITES KILLER.

"It appears the news chaps are going to get every bit of mileage out of this that they can. Turn on the telly." There was a screen in practically every room of their house, so Michael wasn't worried about her not being near one. Michael grimaced as he watched film footage of last night's crowd in the alley behind the theater.

"They're interviewing Liam McKenna," Molly said.

Michael shook his head. "Getting the Big Nick Berryhill story out there, is he?"

"Apparently McKenna's repertoire has now extended to ghosts from the '39 train wreck haunting Blackpool."

"I've never heard of those before."

"He's a self-aggrandizing ass."

"Some people would say that's the very description of an entrepreneur, love. I myself have upon occasion been accused of such behavior."

Molly chuckled and the gentle sound made Michael

smile again and miss her even more. "There's a big difference. I love and forgive you."

"Well, then. That makes it all better." Michael walked
to the window overlooking the front of the house.

Everything seemed less scary in the daylight and the
uneasiness that had followed him up from the gates last
night had nearly gone away. The feeling was as thin as the
fog drifting through the trees in the direction of the bay.
But like the fog, it hadn't entirely disappeared.

"I don't see your car." Michael let the curtain drop and
his stomach tightened a little in apprehension.

"I'm still here at the house." Molly sighed. "Trying to
sort this office into something I can live with."

Some of the tension went away and Michael wished it
all had. He didn't like the idea of worrying about Molly
because that made him overprotective. That wouldn't be
good for either of them and he was wise enough to know
that. Still, the murder and the break-in at their home kept
cycling through his thoughts.

"Need help?"

"Your help?" Molly laughed derisively. "I've seen the
pit you work in."

"Hey." Still, Michael didn't protest. Although his office
had a system to it, there wasn't much in the way of orga-
nization that an outsider might recognize. He knew where
everything was, though, and that was all that mattered.

"No, thank you. The offer is appreciated, but you've
got work of your own to tend to. Making Keith's mermaids more Family Channel than Adults-only, if memory
serves."

Michael gazed at the nearly unrumpled side of the bed
that was Molly's. "Did you sleep last night?"

"A few hours."

Guilt crept in. He hadn't even noticed when she'd gotten up. "Perhaps I can make us some breakfast."

"Iris took care of it earlier. Breakfast was delightful."

"I know Irwin would have also been up early despite the late hour last night." The caretaker was a workaholic, as bad as any of the video-game programmers Michael had ever met. Michael worked that way himself at various times on a project, but he didn't function like clockwork. Sometimes Irwin seemed more than human.

"Of course. The limo has already been cleaned and put away. He's been out this morning investigating the possibility of enhancing the security. But, if you shower and become civilized again, I'd welcome a chance to watch you eat breakfast."

"I'll be down in a moment."

A window opened on the plasma television monitor. The security system they'd chosen was wired to show any visitors at the gates, whether they rang or tripped an alarm. In a second, the window was filled with the image of a man sitting at the gates in a luxury vehicle. He wore a suit, but he was built like a bull mastiff.

"We have company." Michael picked up the television remote.

"I see. I'm at my computer. Do you recognize him?"

"No. I think I know the car, though." He brought up the audio speaker on the television. "May I help you?"

The driver leaned out of the car. Morning light fell across his scarred face and thick features. "Mr. Aleister Crowe for Mrs. Graham, please."

Michael muted the audio. "Were you expecting Crowe?"

"If I were, I'd have said something."

Michael was tempted to tell the man to leave, but he was intrigued as to what brought Crowe to their home. The man was a rare visitor, and only showed up when Molly was entertaining, never by himself.

"Fancy a breakfast chat, love?" Michael stared at the grim-faced driver.

"It would be the fastest way to find out what he wants. If we turn him away now, I'd be dying of curiosity. So would you."

"True." Michael resumed the audio and told the driver to pull through, that someone would meet them at the main house. Then he raced for the shower.

CHAPTER EIGHT

"MRS. GRAHAM, MR. CROWE is here to see you."

Molly stood at the entrance to the breakfast nook, dressed for the day in jeans and a sweater. Judging from Aleister Crowe's dismissive gaze, he wasn't impressed.

Crowe wore a black Saville Row suit and carried his namesake silver-headed cane in one hand and a hat in the other. His coat hung across his shoulders and made him resemble even more the predatory bird his family name was derived from.

They exchanged quick and polite good mornings, then Molly asked him if he'd like tea in the nook. He agreed.

Irwin took Crowe's coat and hat and disappeared with them, but Molly knew that the caretaker wouldn't go far. Irwin didn't care for Aleister Crowe any more than Michael did.

The breakfast nook was a large sunroom. On the north side of the house, the room benefited from steady light without facing either sunrise or sunset. Potted plants hung from the ceiling and sat on the floor. Large bookshelves filled one wall, stocked with books she and Michael treasured, a fireplace another, and floor-to-ceiling windows finished the other two walls.

Molly loved the room. Whenever she felt the need to get away from everything but didn't want to leave the house, she came here. Iris had already put a fresh flower arrangement from the greenhouse on the small, intimate table surrounded by four captain's chairs.

"Charming." Crowe pulled out one of the chairs for Molly.

She thanked him and sat, then waited while he took a chair across from her. "I like it."

"Where is your husband?"

"He will be joining us momentarily."

"Good." Crowe said that as if he meant it, but the tension in his words told Molly that he didn't. She was a good judge of lies and liars, and Crowe was one of the best liars she'd ever met. "That will make things easier."

"What things, Mr. Crowe?"

Crowe smiled but with precious little mirth. "You Americans. You really go straight for the jugular, don't you? Don't sort out the niceties beforehand."

"I would have thought your showing up here this morning precluded all that. Evidently you believed you had something compelling to say or you wouldn't have come."

"Touché, Mrs. Graham."

"Perhaps it would be best if we got to it."

Crowe frowned and his eyebrows knitted into a black slash above his dark eyes. "I think your little endeavor regarding this train robbery has stirred up more ghosts than you'd counted on."

"Why would it do that?"

"That robbery was…very complicated. It had rather severe repercussions."

"It was also seventy years ago. Other than providing the subject for an interesting documentary, I don't see those repercussions could still be relevant today."

"Yet Simon Wineguard saw fit to mention the possibility of treasure."

"Stories are always better if they have treasure in them," Michael said as he strode across the room from the doorway. "Wouldn't you agree, love?" He looked tanned and fit in a pair of cargo pants and a ringer T-shirt. He smiled, then leaned down and kissed Molly on the cheek. "If she owns up to it, something she'll never do unless she's in a mood to, I'm sure my lovely wife will admit that the stories concerning the lost treasures are one of the main reasons she chose to explore this subject with her film crew."

"They're not *my* film crew." Molly raised her coffee cup to mask her smile. She knew Michael had deliberately chosen to dress casually to poke fun at Crowe's stuffy ways.

He took a seat beside her, close but not close enough to intrude on her personal space. Still, the triangle at the table made it clear they were on one side and Crowe was on the other. Michael glanced at Molly. "Has our guest explained his reasons for dropping by?"

"We were just getting to that." Molly sipped her coffee.

Iris brought a new mug to the table and placed it before Michael. He thanked her and poured himself a cup of coffee. He hadn't given up his morning tea, but he had picked up the coffee habit easily enough.

"I assume Paddington warned you to be on your guard." Crowe watched them with a blank face.

"Why?" Michael added cream to his cup.

Crowe locked eyes with him. Molly was intrigued again by how dark Crowe seemed, even sitting in the well-lit room.

"Your unfortunate break-in, of course. Did they get what they were after?" Crowe fisted the silver head of his cane reflexively.

Michael shrugged. "We've found nothing missing."

"Interesting." Crowe's tone indicated that he wasn't overly concerned that none of their possessions had been stolen. "Thieves that break in, then don't steal."

Michael leaned back in his chair. "I appreciate your thoughtfulness in coming here to warn us."

Crowe hesitated, then nodded. "I considered it my civic duty."

A lazy smile played across Michael's lips and Molly couldn't help watching her husband more than Crowe. Michael was a better showman.

"Please excuse me if I appear rude, but I've never known you to be so civic-minded in the past."

If Crowe took offense, he didn't let on. "We're practically neighbors." He swiveled his gaze to Molly. "I did come for another reason, as well, Mrs. Graham. This one concerns you. And the documentary efforts."

"Really? In what regard?"

"Given that poor woman's death, I thought it was possible some of the people who had funded the documentary might try to pull out."

Molly kept her face relaxed. As a matter of fact, she had received two calls so far stating exactly that.

"There has been some anxiety, but I expect it will blow over."

Crowe smiled. "I hope that it does. I understand this project is near and dear to your heart."

Molly decided not to play the man's game. Crowe was more transparent than he believed. "I'm not worried about the documentary, Mr. Crowe. The funding is all in place, and I'm sure that once the initial shock subsides, the investors will see reason and believe in this project again."

"Of course they will, Mrs. Graham." Crowe shrugged and gave her another smile, wider this time. "In the event that some of them decide this situation presents more risks than they can deal with, I'd like to offer my support."

"I appreciate that." Molly returned his smile. She noticed Michael watching her. Her husband's eyes were bright with amusement.

Crowe hesitated for a moment. "I didn't just mean moral support. Though you have that, as well. I was referring to financing your project."

"Really?" Molly was determined not to let Crowe wriggle off the hook so easily. "As I recall, you weren't overly receptive when I sent you a prospectus."

"I've had a change of heart." To the man's credit, he spoke with a straight face and no detectable insincerity.

"All right then. If I need further funding, I'll let you know."

"Excellent." Crowe stood and took a fresh grip on his cane. "Mrs. Graham, thank you for your hospitality. I'll see myself out."

Irwin appeared almost magically in the doorway with Crowe's coat and hat.

Crowe took his things from Irwin, then said his goodbyes and followed the caretaker to the door.

"HAVE I EVER MENTIONED how creepy that man is?" Michael stood at the window overlooking the parking area in front of the main house.

Outside, the burly driver opened the back door of the luxury sedan and allowed Crowe to crawl in. The wind caught the chauffeur's jacket for just a moment, lifting it enough to flash the revolver snugged in a holster on his belt.

"You have." Molly walked to Michael's side. "On several occasions. On that, we agree."

Michael glanced at her as the luxury sedan rolled

sedately toward the front gates. "So what do you think that was all about?"

"That was a fishing expedition. He was trying to ascertain how much of an impression last night made on us."

"My thoughts exactly."

Molly turned away. "I've got to get started. I've done everything here that I can do. Time to get out and make the rounds. See that everyone is settled. Simon hopes to do some of the primary filming in the next few days, but I can't reach him on his mobile. Maybe Joyce Abernathy knows where he is...."

Michael reached out and caught her hand, pulling her back. She looked up at him, her free hand resting on his shoulder as if they were dancing.

"No way, big guy. I've got a full day. You're not going to act all cute and distract me."

Delicately, Michael smoothed her hair behind one ear. "Don't tempt me, love. I can be quite distracting when I choose to be." He smiled playfully, but the effort wasn't completely convincing.

As if sensing his somber mood, Molly touched his chin with a forefinger. "Yes, you can."

"I don't know what's up and about with your project, love. But be careful."

Molly studied him. "Where did all this nervousness come from?"

"It started in the alley last night." Michael felt a chill steal up his spine. "Then the break-in, and Crowe brought more of it this morning. Frankly, it doesn't seem to be going away." He paused. "I just want to make sure you're safe."

"I'm a big girl. My uncle's a detective. I was his favorite niece. He gave me a pair of handcuffs when I was five. I can take care of myself."

"I'd rather you didn't have to take care of yourself."

"My hero." Molly teased him with her smile. Then she glanced at her watch. "Sorry. I've really got to be going. I'll be fine, but if I need you, I'll call. Have fun with your mermaids."

Reluctantly, Michael released her and watched her walk away. He glanced back at the gate where Crowe's car had vanished.

Real life wasn't like a video game. Not everything was a clue. Not everything was foreshadowing of something else. Coincidences—and murders—did happen and didn't touch on anything else.

Michael wasn't happy thinking that. He felt something was missing that was important. He just had no idea what it was.

CHAPTER NINE

THE GOOD THING ABOUT Blackpool's general population depending largely on bicycles and walking to get around was the lack of competition for parking spaces. The downside was that few parking places existed. Thankfully the Blackpool Library had a handful of them tucked at the rear of the building.

Michael parked his dusty Land Rover, got out, stretched, then reached inside for his computer bag. The drive into town wasn't overly long, but he'd gotten knotted up in his thoughts. They'd been more twisted than the shore road and he hadn't had company to keep his mind from obsessing. He felt his back protest after the tension of the drive. He really needed to go for a run or bike ride.

But neither was on his agenda at the moment. He'd tried mucking about with the new game, tinkering with Keith's illustrations, but he hadn't been able to focus on anything other than the train robbery and the potential trouble Molly could find herself in.

The library sat on a hill overlooking the bay. In past days, as Mrs. Hirschfield, the librarian, was fond of saying, there had been a scaffold on the site. For a while it had been used to hang pirates, then to hang those men who hunted pirates. And occasionally whoever else bothered someone in power.

Mrs. Hirschfield wasn't sure when the scaffold had been torn down or what had become of it, but the legend persisted. Liam McKenna often brought tours to the site, and some of the local kids experimented with Ouija boards and séances at night. A few claimed to have seen the dead wandering around the hills.

Michael crossed the crushed-seashell parking area toward the front door. Like the police station, the library had once been a family home and had been remodeled. This house was a lot larger, a rambling affair that was still hard to heat in the winter. Many of the walls had been removed to make bigger rooms, which were then filled with shelving.

Down the hill, the eastern section of Blackpool meandered toward the abbreviated beach dotted with piers and small marinas. Michael paused to admire the view.

Then the door opened and a bell overhead tinkled like breaking glass.

Startled, he turned around and discovered Mrs. Hirschfield standing before him. She was a small gnome of a woman, with a wrinkled face and hair piled on top of her head. Bracelets and bangles bounced on her bony wrists. She peered myopically at Michael through John Lennon glasses, the lenses so thick they almost made her look cross-eyed.

"Mrs. Hirschfield." Michael smiled. "You gave me a bit of a start."

"You were standing there long enough that I wondered if you'd forgotten how to operate the door."

"Just admiring the view."

"I suppose I know what brings you to the library this morning."

"Can't I just stop by and browse?"

The woman smiled politely. "Mr. Graham, you never just stop by and browse. You always have an agenda. You only come here when you can't find answers anywhere else."

Michael supposed that was true. With the Internet and Amazon at his fingertips, there wasn't much reason to visit the library. Despite its attempts to keep currently stocked with new books, the budget was severely lacking. And he liked to own books rather than borrow them.

With a smile, he nodded. "You've got me. I do have an agenda."

"The train robbery in 1940, I gather?"

Taken a little aback, Michael nodded.

Mrs. Hirschfield adjusted her glasses. "Don't act surprised. The whole town is getting treasure fever. It's all nonsense, of course. If there were treasure from that train robbery or any other, it would have been found long before. Those young people and their cave spelunking certainly would have tumbled across it. No, those thieves made off with it all those years ago." She stepped back and waved him inside. "Come in. You're letting the warm air out."

As he crossed the threshold, Michael noticed that the chill that lay over the bay didn't encroach inside the library. He followed the librarian through the adjoining rooms.

"Frankly, I'm surprised you've been taken by treasure fever, Mr. Graham. I would have thought if you were interested, you would have accompanied Mrs. Graham when she visited to do her research."

"Yes, well. I didn't expect to become so personally invested in the documentary."

"Mrs. Whiteshire's death certainly cast things in a different light."

"Yes, it did."

"There are some who believe her death had something to do with the train robbery."

"I rather doubt that."

"What you want is back here." Mrs. Hirschfield led Michael to a back room that was already occupied by library patrons and stacks of bound newspapers. "I've left everything out because so many people kept asking for it."

Michael's heart sank. "You don't have digital copies of the newspapers from those times?"

Mrs. Hirschfield shot him an admonishing look. "We're not like those fancy libraries you're used to in London, Mr. Graham. We're a local library just struggling to get by. When I can put more books on the shelves than I have to throw away, I consider it a good year."

"And well you should." Michael didn't know what else to say, but he decided to pay attention to library donations in the future.

The chairs around the tables offered only the cold, hard promise of straight-backed torture. Most of the people in the room he recognized as townsfolk. A few were likely tourists, maybe camped at the marina. A young brunette with a BBC media bag and uncomfortable-looking high heels regarded him suspiciously.

Michael groaned inwardly. He was used to researching at home. He had a large screen and a SMART Board for when he wanted to think on his feet. There was also a lot more space to spread out the documents.

Michael reached into his computer bag and brought out a small digital camera. He never traveled anywhere without it.

He took a moment, breathing deeply to clear his mind, then removed a notepad and wrote out a list of questions as quickly as he could.

Who knew about the train?
How was it robbed?

Who lost the most?
Who investigated the theft?
Who in Blackpool was involved?

He sighed—it was going to be a long day. He focused and started reading.

MOLLY WAS IN THE COMMON room of the Cavendish House Bed-and-Breakfast, one of the better-appointed establishments in Blackpool, when Miss Abernathy returned from police custody.

The diminutive woman appeared completely out of place in the elegant Victorian stylings of the Cavendish House. Judging from the state of her dress, the wildness of her hair and the hollow circles under her eyes, her stay in the Blackpool jail hadn't agreed with her.

Martha Cavendish, the elderly hotelier, stared at her with a stern glare.

"Miss Abernathy." Molly stepped toward the small woman.

Wheeling like a startled animal, Miss Abernathy focused on Molly. After a couple of blinks, recognition dawned in the woman's eyes and she smiled.

"Ah, Molly." Miss Abernathy took Molly's hands in hers and blew kisses on either side of her cheeks as they embraced. "It is so good to see you. You look fantastic."

Molly didn't bother to return the compliment. She knew from working with Miss Abernathy that the other woman wouldn't buy into any polite lies.

The woman leaned back and peered through one of the windows with a view of Main Street. "I've seen a number of cars in town this morning. I expect that's the BBC?"

Molly nodded. "And a few others."

Miss Abernathy shook her head. "Evidently we've gone

gold after our very public appearance. Our story could be in the news before we get a chance to start shooting the documentary."

"That's not what we want."

"I realize it's not what *we* want." Miss Abernathy scowled. "But it may be the very thing *Simon* wants."

"I would think that was the last thing Simon sought."

Miss Abernathy frowned. "Only a few months ago, I would have agreed. As it turns out, Simon has an agenda all his own."

"What do you mean?"

After a quick glance over her shoulder at the hotelier, Miss Abernathy nodded toward the stairs. "Perhaps it would be better if we talked in my room. This little town has big ears."

CHAPTER TEN

JOYCE ABERNATHY CROSSED her small bedroom to the tiny window overlooking Blackpool's downtown area. She brushed aside the curtains bearing bright yellow roses and opened the window.

"I hate being closed up. Having to deal with the metal stink of the jail and that hard cot was horrible." The woman sat on the window seat and waved Molly to the rocking chair across from the neatly made bed.

Molly sat, taking in the nautical theme reflected by a ship-in-a-bottle lamp, paintings of tall ships and carved figurines of fish on the television stand.

"I assume someone in the Cavendish family was a seaman." Miss Abernathy touched the ship's lantern that had been converted into a lamp over the tiny writing desk.

"A captain, actually. Mrs. Cavendish's husband still captains a fishing boat."

She gave her first smile. "It's a lovely place to stay."

Molly had arranged the accommodations for both Miss Abernathy and Simon, although Simon had elected to room somewhere else. "I'm glad you think so," Molly said. "When Simon stated that he'd rather not stay here, I was surprised."

"He was just being difficult. I don't think he realized Blackpool didn't have a true hotel until our arrival."

"Then why did he object to the lodging?"

"He enjoys being the prima donna from time to time. It feeds his ego." Miss Abernathy grimaced. "That big, fat, pompous ego of his."

Surprised at the other woman's intense—and negative—emotion, Molly remained silent. During the times she'd spent with Simon Wineguard and Miss Abernathy, Molly had only seen the two act like a well-oiled machine.

Embarrassment flitted across Miss Abernathy's face. "Honestly, Molly, can you see anything different from this bed-and-breakfast and the Seagull and Sandbar, where he's currently staying?"

"This is a more picturesque place, in my opinion."

Miss Abernathy nodded. "It is. The key difference for Simon is that there's a pub across the street from the Seagull and Sandbar."

Molly waited politely for Miss Abernathy to get back to the real issue at hand.

"I loved your idea of the Operation Pied Piper story, Molly. Truly, I did. But that wasn't what drew Simon here to Blackpool."

"I'm afraid I don't understand."

"Simon wants to do the documentary, as he's told you. But he has an ulterior motive, as well. You've heard of the Sterling family?"

"Yes. One of the children lost aboard the train was Chloe Sterling."

"What do you know about the family?"

Molly recalled the material she'd gone over when pulling the presentation about the documentary together. "They were wealthy and influential. Involved in a number of businesses, mostly shipping and some industrial concerns like canning and furniture manufacturing. Lived in London. Chloe was the sole heir of the eldest Sterling, Richard. After the war the family fell on hard times."

"I knew you'd done your homework." Miss Abernathy smiled. "In many ways, you remind me of myself. Chloe Sterling's unfortunate end was a sad story. Richard Sterling passed away shortly after his daughter's passing. They say he died of a broken heart. He was a widower. Chloe's mother died in childbirth. Until I learned of the tale of the train robbery, I'd heard nothing but bad things about the family."

"What bad things?"

"After Richard died in 1941, his brother Edward took over the family fortune. There was talk that he was helping the Nazis during the war. Nothing could ever be proven, though. The war occupied everyone's attention, and there's no evidence Edward Sterling was ever a Nazi sympathizer. He just didn't mind making money from the Germans. He fancied himself his own private Switzerland and supplied both sides with supplies and munitions." She paused. "At least, that's what Simon believes."

"Even if that were true, that was seventy years ago. What does it have to do with the documentary?"

"Because Simon is hoping to leverage the Operation Pied Piper film to pursue his next project—an exposé of the Sterling family and their ties to criminal syndicates." Miss Abernathy shifted on the window seat. "Simon ended up crossways with Bartholomew Sterling—he's the current head of the family, son to Edward Sterling—over a woman, I think. I don't quite have all the particulars, but Simon has had it in for Bartholomew Sterling for years."

Molly considered that. "Simon came here under false pretenses?"

"Not exactly." Miss Abernathy sighed. "This is hard to explain correctly because I feel betrayed, as well." She knotted a fist in her lap. "Simon should have told me what he'd planned right from the start."

"When did he tell you?"

"Last night. After that poor woman had been murdered. And then the police were asking me so many questions. I knew if I relayed to the police anything he'd said to me it would only make Simon look guilty. Little did I realize that keeping silent only made *me* look guilty, and all I got for my loyalty was a night in jail. And Simon? Simon was *excited.*"

"About the murder?"

"Not about that. He felt horrible that she was killed. Responsible even. But he said her murder was proof that he needed to bring the Sterling family to its knees."

"He believes the Sterlings had something to do with the murder? But why would they have any interest in Abigail Whiteshire?"

Miss Abernathy pushed herself to her feet and kicked off her heels. She began to pace the small room in her stocking feet.

"Simon is convinced they were sending him a message."

"A message."

Miss Abernathy nodded. "A warning."

"About what?"

"Simon thinks they know he's planning to do a documentary about them and their association with the mob. After the war, even though the rumors of consorting with the Nazis couldn't be verified, Edward Sterling was ostracized by the London elite. For a while, the family's standing dropped dramatically. People stayed away from their businesses. Edward started working with some of the East End criminal organizations. Slowly, he built his fortune back up. Ultimately, though, the ties with the criminal organizations got tighter."

"None of that ever turned up in my research."

As she considered the matter, Molly thought about the men who had invaded her home. To get past all of the high-tech security Michael had had installed in the home, the burglars were professionals. And professionals were expensive.

"But did you ever take a hard look at the Sterling family in your research?" Miss Abernathy asked.

"There was no need. They weren't the story. The film was going to be about what happened to those children."

"For you, yes. But not for Simon. The Sterling connection is the only story he's after."

"Does he think they had anything to do with the train robbery?"

"No. Remember, Richard Sterling was still alive then. He was simply trying to protect his daughter by getting her out of London. And to help save all those women and children."

"Have you talked with Simon this morning?"

"No. When I was released from jail, he was nowhere to be found. I tried his mobile, but he's not answering."

"Have you checked his B and B?"

"I did. I went there first."

Concern gnawed at Molly. "Did Inspector Paddington know where he might be?"

"I didn't ask. I assumed Simon would be in his room."

"Perhaps I should search for him. Blackpool isn't so big that I can't find him."

"I would offer to go with you, but I'm in no mood to see him right now. I think he might feel the same way about me." Miss Abernathy's expression grew stern. "We get like this every now and again. I'm sorry you've been caught in the middle of it, Molly. It's not fair to you."

"I'll be fine. Trust me, I've weathered much worse." Molly could see Simon's assistant was exhausted. "You should get some rest. We'll have a lot to deal with in light of everything that went on last night, but first I'll track down Simon."

Miss Abernathy regarded Molly wistfully. "When you do, could you call me and let me know? I just want to know that he's all right. He's really not himself when the Sterling family is involved."

"Of course." Molly stood and walked toward the door. "Try to get some rest. I'll be in touch as soon as I can."

Outside the Cavendish House, Molly slid on her sunglasses, and clicked open the doors of her silver Mini Cooper with her keys. After she buckled in and started the engine, she pulled her iPhone from her handbag and switched on the wireless function. She spoke Michael's name and the speaker system broadcast the ring tone as she pulled out onto the street.

"Hello, love." Michael's voice sounded sexy and filled with suggestive promise. "Miss me?"

Molly smiled. "Always. Keeping yourself occupied?"

"Not with a game, though."

"Really?"

"I swear. I'm at the Blackpool Library."

"Researching train robberies?" Molly glided to a stop at one of the town's few stop signs and checked both ways. When she glanced up, she spotted a Blackpool police cruiser traveling a short distance behind her.

"As a matter of fact, I am. As you knew I would be."

"I knew you wouldn't be able to resist." Molly checked the rearview mirror a moment longer. The two policemen in the cruiser behind her tried to look at everything but her. "Actually, if you're not too busy today, there is a favor I have to ask of you."

"Oh? Something strenuous, I hope."

"You realize that these mobile signals bleed over onto maritime radios."

"Embarrassed?"

"Not yet." Molly started forward again. The police car stayed with her. "About the favor. Could you research Bartholomew Sterling for me?"

"Ah. The nephew of Richard Sterling."

"You *have* been doing your homework."

"I excel at research, love. As you are well aware of. Why the interest in Bartholomew Sterling?"

Molly quickly brought Michael up-to-date on Simon Wineguard's interest in the man.

"You realize you only have Miss Abernathy's word to go on."

"I do. But I keep thinking about Mrs. Whiteshire. The killers shot her, then broke into her house using her key. That doesn't sound like a typical mugging to me."

"Nor to me." Michael hummed at the other end of the line. It was something he did when he was deep in thought, though he wasn't aware of it. The sound pleased Molly and made her smile. When Michael was humming, his mind was fully engaged.

"And there is the matter of the breach in our security."

"Agreed. I don't think Blackpool has the necessary criminal talent to do that." Michael took a deep breath. "While I'm here researching, what are you going to be doing?"

"I'm trying to find Simon Wineguard."

"Gone missing, has he?"

"For the moment. Miss Abernathy suggested that he might be in his rooms. Or at a pub." Molly glanced in the rearview mirror. The police cruiser was still there. "Would you believe that Inspector Paddington is having his men follow me around?"

"No." Concern tightened Michael's voice. "But I have to admit that I'm not terribly surprised. The break-in last night left an impression on us, and I'm betting the inspector was also suitably impressed." He paused. "Be careful, love. This is already shaping up to be a nasty bit of business and I would feel much better if you were well clear of it."

"I'll be careful." For a moment, Molly felt a chill as she remembered the dead woman lying in the street. "I'd just hoped that the murder was not connected to us in any way."

"Me, too."

"But you don't think that's true, either. That's why you're at the library this morning."

He sighed. She knew him too well sometimes. "Yes."

"Find out what you can about Bartholomew Sterling."

"I will, and when I do, is there some kind of prize involved?"

"Perhaps."

Michael chuckled. "Tease. In the meantime, what happens when you finally corner Simon?"

"He's going to fess up to his real intentions regarding this documentary."

"I almost feel sorry for him."

Laughing, Molly disconnected the call.

CHAPTER ELEVEN

BLACKPOOL MOVED AT A LAZY morning pace. Weekend tourists who had arrived by boat wandered through the shops and restaurants. Glower Lighthouse stood tall out in the harbor. Festive sails belled and caught the wind, powering boats out to sea.

The police cruiser rolled to a stop behind Molly as she opened the door and got out. She walked back to the uniformed officers, conscious of the stares she drew from the townsfolk.

"Good morning, gentlemen." Molly smiled at them and peered at the name badge on the driver. "Officer Fotherby."

"Constable." The big man raked a hand over his stubbled chin. The rasp of his beard cut through the purr of the car's idling engine. "Constable Fotherby."

"Back home we call policemen officers." Molly folded her arms. "Would you like to tell me why you're following me?"

A flash of irritation shadowed Fotherby's face. "Mrs. Graham, you're blocking traffic."

Molly looked around the street. Gawkers stood around, watching what was happening. No other cars moved along the thoroughfare.

"I don't believe I'm blocking traffic, Constable Fotherby." Molly kept her voice calm, professional, but she knew there was a hint of ice in her words.

Fotherby swiveled his gaze onto her with laser intensity, then upped the wattage. Molly supposed if she was the type to be easily intimidated, that would have done the trick.

"Perhaps you'd appreciate a ticket this fine morning, Mrs. Graham."

"I'd protest it in court, Constable. And then things would turn ugly."

The other man leaned over to Fotherby. He was older, smaller and slimmer, with a neatly cut mustache and gray hair. "Let it go, mate. The inspector knew we weren't going to exactly be on stealth mode for this bit."

Fotherby shrugged off the other constable's words without breaking eye contact with Molly. "I've got my orders, Mrs. Graham. The inspector says we're supposed to stay with you."

"Why?"

"For your own protection."

Molly crossed her arms. "Really?"

"Yes, ma'am." The other constable answered while Fotherby continued trying to stare Molly down. "Because of the murder last night. And the break-ins. Inspector Paddington considers it a wise precaution."

"Thank you, Constable. The inspector might have mentioned that."

"He didn't want to worry you, ma'am."

Fotherby cursed. "Don't talk to her, Wallingham."

"I'll talk to who I like, when I like, Fotherby."

Molly focused on the older constable. "I assume I'm not the only one the inspector is having tailed."

"Ma'am, I'm not at liberty to say what the inspector is doing."

Thank goodness for all that grant money I secured for additional police officers during the documentary. "I'm looking for Simon Wineguard. If you could point me to him, I want to speak with him. That way you'll have two of us in one place and you won't have to follow me all around Blackpool while I search for him. Perhaps one of your teams could go for coffee. Or tea."

"We're not here to plug your social calendar." Fotherby slipped on a pair of sunglasses with mirror lenses. They gave him a cold, insectoid appearance.

"I'm trying to make this easier on all of us," Molly said. "Otherwise you'll spend the day staring at my tailgate as I have no idea where Simon is." She couldn't believe the man's stubbornness.

"Wineguard's at the marina." Wallingham referred to a small notepad from his pocket. "On a yacht called *Crystal Dancer.* Slip P-62."

Fotherby gripped the steering wheel more tightly and stared through the windshield as if he weren't a part of the conversation.

"Thank you, Constable Wallingham."

Wallingham touched the brim of his short-billed cap and gave her a small smile. "You're welcome, ma'am."

"I suppose you'll be along after me."

"Yes, ma'am."

Molly cut her gaze to the younger constable. "I'll try not to lose you."

Fotherby growled a curse.

Molly turned and strode back to her car. She thought about Inspector Paddington's interest and wondered where it was coming from. It was probably an overreaction— except for the break-ins and the "mugging" gone bad.

Of course, there was also the possibility that Inspector Paddington had discovered Simon Wineguard's connection to the Sterling family. Before coming to Blackpool, Paddington had worked in London's Metro unit.

Behind the wheel, Molly buckled herself in and made

an illegal U-turn, flouting the law deliberately to get under Fotherby's skin. She didn't care for the man or his attitude. In the rearview mirror, the police cruiser's lights came on and Molly wondered if she'd pushed the situation too far.

The two constables argued for a moment, then the lights went off. A moment later, they trailed behind her at a sedate pace.

MICHAEL STUDIED THE photographs of the train wreck in the microfiche files as he nursed a cup of tea. The robbers hadn't mucked about in their efforts to stop the train. According to the story, they had felled trees to block the tracks around a curve only a few miles outside of Blackpool. When the train had ground to a stop in the forest, the robbers had triggered an explosive charge under the pulling engine as the engineer tried to reverse.

The explosion overturned the pulling engine and coal car and ripped them apart. The engineer and fireman had died in the blast, as well as several passengers.

Quietly, Michael surveyed the black-and-white images and imagined what those frantic moments must have been like. The line of cars had buckled and become a broken-backed snake. Carnage spread out from the tracks and into the forest. According to reports, passengers—including the children—were strewn across the landscape.

The gold bullion shipment had carried extra guards—a military attachment. Unfortunately, most of them were new recruits and hadn't ever been under fire. They'd responded to the attack, according to interviews with survivors, but hadn't been able to stand up to the intense fire of the robbers' machine guns and heavy rifle barrage.

Some of the photographs showed the damage close up. Michael analyzed the huge holes punched through the railway cars. An army liaison had speculated that the robbers had used Browning automatic rifles in the attack. They were heavy, but men could carry them easily enough.

Blackpool Police Constable Henry Mullins had been shocked and appalled, according to the reporter. "Those weapons were designed as tank killers. Taking cover in those railcars would have been about as effective as taking refuge in a sardine tin. The guards never had a chance. This was a cold-blooded killing. Executions, the lot of them."

The report was long and filled with details, including the fact that the car holding the paintings hadn't been fired upon at all. When the reporter had questioned the military liaison about whether the robbers had to have had inside information, the army representative had dodged the question.

Michael was fascinated by the logistics of the train heist, as well as the mystery. Although a part of him was horrified at the loss of life.

And the children. He shivered in the room and wondered if the people around him reading the reports were equally moved.

The biggest mystery of the robbery was how the thieves had transported the stolen items out of the area. Moving that much gold would have been difficult under any conditions, let alone in the middle of the forest outside a small town with few routes of escape.

Michael picked up his pen and notepad, thinking how he would have handled the situation if he had been in charge of the robbery. Not that he would ever kill anyone.

Still, as a game designer he planned a lot of complex and intricate puzzles. Sometimes he wondered if he'd become too coldly analytical because of it. Then he realized how sickened he'd been while looking at the photographs and had empathized with the victims for what they'd been forced to endure.

He shelved his emotions for the moment and gave his attention over to the problem.

CHAPTER TWELVE

OUT IN THE DISTANCE, A THIN fog drifted in patches over the harbor. The slate-gray sea seemed to lift up like the edge of a bowl to meet the dulled cotton of the sky. Only the bright sails of pleasure craft riding the ocean waves brought any color to the scene.

An elderly man in faded blue coveralls stood guard over the marina gate. He watched Molly as she walked along the pier. Her heels clacked against the rough wood.

The marina was old and in need of refurbishing. Many of the buildings, warehouses and offices were weathered and gray. Almost all of the color had drained away, leeched out by the sun and the constant damp. Seagulls and terns flocked across the pier, the boats' and ships' rigging, and the buoys that marked the various sections of the harbor.

"Can I help you, mum?" The man stood on the other side of the locked gate, a Members Only sign prominently welded to the wrought iron. Molly noticed the knife and net scars on his hands, and then saw he held a new shiny black walkie-talkie.

"I'm a member." Molly took her identification card from her handbag and showed it to the man. She and Michael kept a cabin cruiser at the marina.

The man looked at the card. Gray stubble knotted his lined cheeks. "Your boat ain't docked here, mum."

"No. I'm here to see a friend on the *Crystal Dancer*."

With a nod, he returned Molly's identification card.

"Yes, mum. We just have to be careful. Got a lot of strangers in town right now, and there's all manner of things going on."

"I understand." Molly waited till the man unlocked the gate, then strode through. The wind whipped around her, chilling her and filling her nostrils with the brine smell of the sea and the odor of decomposing fish.

On the docks, fishermen worked their hauls. Heavy blades chopped through tuna and other fish with meaty thunks against the thick wooden slabs. Nets hung from rigging, some of it still dripping water in machine gun–fire drips. Pop music and hardcore rock warred with the cries of the gulls and terns.

Molly felt out of place around the fishermen. She always did. Michael, on the other hand, could mix in with anyone, including the close-mouthed individuals that mined the sea for a living. On occasion, he had gone with some of the men for a day or two at a time when the fish were running. He loved new experiences and so far she hadn't seen him turn away from anything.

But she enjoyed the atmosphere of the area. The marina and the harbor always summoned up images of Blackpool's past. All she had to do was gaze off in the distance and she could imagine pirate ships and privateers sailing into port.

Michael, too, was fascinated by the legends of the place. History always seemed to call out to him and hurl his imagination into overdrive.

But Molly had fallen in love with the romance and mystery of the town. So many stories yet remained to be told.

Like the one about the train robbery in 1940.

Crystal Dancer sat at anchorage near the end of the

dock. The boat's position told Molly that she was a visitor to the area—a resident would have had a closer berth.

The boat was a sixty-footer, sleek and clean. She rode the water well, balanced and poised. Her white hull had yellow and blue stripes that appeared freshly painted.

Molly followed the narrow planking that ran alongside the boat. Farther out, the pier stretched uneasily, more at the mercy of the sea as it swayed atop shifting pilings.

"Hello?" Molly gazed up at the yacht.

A man in dress whites sauntered over to the side in a rolling gait that offered mute testimony that he'd spent years at sea. He looked like he was in his late thirties or early forties, handsome and clean cut.

"Good morning," he called down from the railing.

"My name is Molly Graham. I'm here to talk with Simon Wineguard, if he's available."

"What business do you have with Mr. Wineguard?" The smile remained in place and the man maintained his polite demeanor.

"Just give him my name, please."

"Aye, ma'am. I'll see if Mr. Wineguard is aboard."

"If you were any kind of ship's crew, I'd think you'd know that without having to check."

For a moment she feared the man had taken offense at her words, then his smile spread. "Aye, ma'am. I suppose you're right." He slipped a cell phone from his pocket and made a call. After a brief conversation, he put the phone away and returned his focus to Molly. "If you'll move over a bit, I'll run out a gangplank and we'll pipe you up. As it happens, we do have a Mr. Wineguard aboard. Perhaps it's *your* Mr. Wineguard."

"Wouldn't that be fortuitous?" Molly didn't bother to curb her sarcasm. She took a couple steps away.

The man maneuvered a metal gangplank onto the pier,

bridging the expanse of sea between the berth wall and the boat's hull. Black friction patches on the gangplank provided a more sure-footed passage.

Molly walked up, conscious of her heels.

"Mr. Wineguard and Miss Roderick are downstairs in the salon," the man said as she stepped on board. He pulled the gangplank back up and put it away.

"You told them I was here?"

"Aye, ma'am." The sailor tugged on his short-billed cap. "I'm Hugh Dorrance, captain of this vessel. Now, if you'll follow me, I'll take you to Mr. Wineguard and Miss Roderick."

"MOLLY?" SIMON SAT ON A PLUSH white couch across from an attractive young woman who Molly judged to be in her mid to late twenties.

The cabin was as elegant and fully outfitted as a living room in a house. Only the stainless-steel galley and numerous windows on the wall gave away its true nature. The couch formed a horseshoe around an equally white low table.

"Good morning, Simon." Molly focused on the woman seated across from the director. "I didn't mean to interrupt, but I wanted to speak with you as soon as possible. You weren't returning my calls or Miss Abernathy's. I thought something might have happened to your mobile."

The woman spoke. "It's no interruption, Mrs. Graham." She was beautiful and self-assured. Bone-white hair cascaded across her bare shoulders. Pale blue eyes held a rounded innocence that Molly just couldn't bring herself to believe in. Her body was long and lithe, that of an athlete, and she wore designer jeans tucked into chocolate calf-high boots, and a chocolate scoopneck blouse. A silver and sapphire-clustered necklace looped in the hollow of her throat.

"Thank you."

Flowing to her feet effortlessly, the woman offered a hand. "Evidently Simon has lost all sense of manners. I'm Synthia Roderick. It's a pleasure to meet you, Mrs. Graham. Simon has told me a lot about you."

"You have a very lovely boat, Miss Roderick."

"Call me Syn. Everyone does. Please sit. Would you like some tea to take the chill off?"

"Thank you. And you can call me Molly." Stepping into the sunken living room area, Molly sunk into one end of the horseshoe-shaped couch, across from Syn Roderick.

Syn nodded and sat back down, curling her booted legs under her. Almost immediately a young woman in kitchen whites brought over a cup and an individual teapot and placed them in front of Molly.

Molly glanced at Simon and saw the director was somewhat at a loss for words. He appeared irritated and nervous at the same time.

"How did you find me?"

"It seems Inspector Paddington is having us both followed."

"He's what?" Simon cursed and looked more anxious. He pulled at his lower lip with his thumb and forefinger.

Syn grinned impishly and cocked an eyebrow at Simon. "The police are tailing you?"

"Yes." Molly was disturbed by the reaction of Syn and Simon. What did Simon have to be worried about? And there was certainly nothing amusing about the events that had triggered Paddington's interest.

"Did the police follow you here?" Simon had paled a little.

"One of the constables trailing me told me where you were."

Syn laughed then. "Delicious. Your little production is definitely going to get a lot more press than you'd expected, Simon."

With a scowl, Simon shook his head and glared at the young woman. "This isn't good, Syn. Not good at all."

"Why? What are we doing wrong? Nothing, that's what." She dipped a finger in her drink, swirled it about, then sucked the liquid off. "You're so negative, Simon."

We? Molly noted the plural pronoun and immediately wondered about that. If Synthia Roderick was involved in the documentary, Molly should have known. She shifted her attention to Simon. "Why isn't it good?"

Simon shrugged, but the effort wasn't relaxed or nonchalant. "I don't want to be distracted during the filming. That's all."

Syn tapped her glass with an elegant fingernail, still smiling. "I would think the death of that unfortunate woman would already be a big distraction. Especially if it's connected to your documentary."

"It's not connected. And this is not something to be so carefree about." Simon drained his drink. He held up the glass and the uniformed woman immediately came for it.

"Does the inspector believe the woman's death was tied to our film?" Syn studied Molly.

"I don't know. Inspector Paddington plays things very close to the vest."

"In a town this small," she said, "the police would be stressed to capacity tailing people. Not to mention keeping track of all the media types turning over rocks for a story."

"The police seem up to the task at the moment." Molly didn't bother to explain. "Did I interrupt anything?"

Simon accepted a fresh drink from the young woman. Given the glaze over his eyes, Molly was sure he'd been drinking more than he should have.

"Not at all." Syn set her glass aside. The attendant came forward to remove it, then hesitated. Syn waved her off. "Just two old friends catching up."

Molly didn't buy the "friends" act. Simon was easily twice Synthia Roderick's age.

"Syn is practically family." Simon nodded at the young woman. "I knew her parents quite well."

"I've always thought of Simon as a doting uncle." She favored him with a smile.

"Are you going to be in Blackpool long?" Molly asked.

Syn shrugged. "It depends on how busy Simon gets with his work. I bore easily. I own this boat and the crew is full-time. I travel wherever and whenever I wish."

And you wished to be here today. "Doesn't sound boring."

"Trust me, I avoid boring whenever I can."

Simon cleared his throat. "Was there anything you needed, Molly?"

Molly considered confronting Simon with Joyce Abernathy's suspicions about Simon's true motives for doing the documentary. But she was reluctant to do that in front of Syn, or while Simon was intoxicated. She shook her head. "I just wanted to make sure you were all right."

"I am."

"And to make sure we're on track to begin shooting principal footage tomorrow."

Simon nodded. "Provided we can keep the media away." He pointed toward Syn with his glass. "Privacy is the chief reason I took Syn up on her invitation to come visit. I wasn't getting much at the B and B. And my mobile kept ringing. That's why I finally turned it off."

"Not having a mobile number to reach you at could be problematic." Molly clamped down her irritation at Simon's lack of consideration.

Syn scooped up a Lana Marks silver crocodile bag, easily worth six figures, and drew a business card from it. The card was surprisingly simple but heavily embossed and perfumed. It read SYN and gave her mobile number.

"If you have trouble getting Simon, you can call me. I plan on keeping up with him over the next few days. At least until the circus goes away."

"Thank you." Molly put the card in her own clutch and stood to go. "You were aware, Simon, that Miss Abernathy spent the night in the Blackpool jail because she was trying to protect you?"

Simon hesitated, then scratched his chin. "I thought she would only have been questioned a bit by the inspector."

"She didn't get out till this morning."

"How sad for her," Syn said. "Jail can be *so* boring."

Personal experience? Molly barely restrained herself from asking the question.

"I'm sure she's all right." Simon waved his hand dismissively. "During the years of our association, Miss Abernathy has always proven herself to be resourceful."

"Despite last night, she's concerned about you," Molly said.

Simon let out a labored breath. "She's loyal. She's always been extremely loyal. That's gotten her into trouble before, I'm afraid." He gave her a brief smile. "But if there's anything else you need, Molly, feel free to call that mobile number. I'll be in touch."

Knowing she'd been dismissed, Molly said her goodbyes and left, angrier than when she'd arrived. And she was very disturbed by the sudden change in Simon Wineguard.

CHAPTER THIRTEEN

"HELLO, LOVE."

Michael stood in one corner of the Blackpool library near a model replica of the town as he spoke to Molly on his mobile. Near as he could be certain, the model was over two hundred years old.

Several of the buildings had changed over the intervening centuries, but Glower Lighthouse, Crowe's Nest—the ancestral home of Charles Crowe—Widow's Peak, the library and the house where the police department had taken up residence all stood out. The firehouse was even on the same block, except that in the model the fire brigade was depicted with horse-drawn wagons instead of modern engines. Tall-masted ships stood in the harbor.

Each time he'd come to the library, Michael had been drawn to the model. It was one of the most intricately designed creations he'd ever seen and he couldn't imagine the amount of time that had gone into its construction. The man who had painstakingly built the miniature town had to have been obsessed. According to the small brass plaque, it was Charles Crowe, the Crowe family patriarch, who had done the work himself back in the eighteenth century. Michael doubted that and wondered if there had been a collaborator somewhere along the way.

But then, Blackpool was a town founded on secrets. As a pirate port, the residents had jealously guarded their vices and crimes. Michael hadn't been able to get any straight information about the ruins of Ravenhearst Manor or what had happened to its owner—Emma Ravenhearst. Puzzles bothered him till he solved them—but he had enough puzzles to deal with without adding Emma Ravenhearst and a ghost to the mix.

"I hope you're having a better day than I am." Molly sounded vexed.

"Did you locate your wayward director?" Michael leaned against the glass case housing the model and looked out into the harbor. Only a few remnants of the fog remained.

"I did. Not where I'd expected. It seems he's got new lodgings with an old friend I hadn't known about. If it wasn't for Paddington's men, I might not have found him till he was ready to be found."

"It's good to know that they're capable. Is Simon hiding out?"

"Not especially. But he didn't seem thrilled to see me."

"I can't imagine anyone having that reaction to you."

"You're sweet."

Michael shifted as he transferred his gaze back to the tiny town. "I can understand Simon trying to get away from the media."

"Have you ever heard of Synthia Roderick?"

He could hear the sound of her car starting.

"Syn?"

"Michael, do *not* tell me you know her."

"Ah…we've met, love. Nothing more. She was interested in investing in the game studio a couple of years before I met you."

"Are you sure that was all she was interested in?"

Michael reflected on the evening he'd spent with Syn Roderick and thought perhaps there were some things it was best to keep Molly in the dark about. Syn had made it clear that she found him very appealing and she hadn't been easily convinced that the "appeal" wasn't mutual.

"She's a flighty one, love. Definitely not my cup of tea. Why did you ask about her?"

"Simon's with her. She has a very large boat, *Crystal Dancer,* out in the harbor."

"Interesting." Michael took his finger back from the glass display case. "Blackpool isn't a place she'd just happen by."

"She didn't just 'happen by.' She came to see Simon. As I said, apparently they're old friends."

"Aha... Well, I've got news, too. I researched the Sterling family," Michael said. "I've found out some things that I'm curious about. Is it close enough to lunch that we could get together and talk?"

"Sure. I'll meet you at the Smokehouse."

LOCATED ON BELL STREET, the Smokehouse stood three stories tall and offered seating on verandas around the second and third floor. Patio dining was available on a flagstone addition in the alley between it and the clothing shop next door. Most patrons preferred the scenic views from the upper floors.

Molly sat at a small table near the railing overlooking Bell Street. Brass bell-shaped torches lined the narrow street and gleamed in the noonday sun. The day had warmed up considerably and she sat without a coat, basking in the rays. Idly, she straightened the yellow rose in the table setting.

"Put that between your teeth, love, and this will be one of those lunches I've always dreamed of."

Glancing up, Molly spotted Michael winding through the close-set tables toward her. He had his leather jacket flung over one shoulder. His casual dress of jeans, black soccer jersey and amber aviator sunglasses made him seem rugged.

"All manly and you brought a jacket?" Molly smiled at him.

Michael leaned in for a kiss, then hung the jacket over the back of his chair and sat. "I brought the jacket for you. In case you get a chill."

"You've got a good heart, Michael Graham." Molly folded her arms and looked at him. "Syn Roderick."

"So that's the way it's to be, eh?"

"I'm curious."

The waitress approached the table and set a pot of tea in front of Michael and a cup of hot chocolate before Molly.

"I took the liberty of ordering for us." Molly sipped the hot chocolate delicately so she wouldn't scald her tongue. "You're having lobster. I'm having fish. I thought we could share."

"Brilliant." Michael shifted in his chair and got comfortable. "Syn Roderick is from old money. Her parents died in a plane wreck while she was in college and she assumed control of the family businesses. Mostly she contents herself to staying out of the boardrooms and letting her majordomos run the corporations. And getting as much ink in the tabloids as possible."

"But occasionally she takes an interest."

Michael nodded. "She does. Generally she tries to acquire new industries outside the periphery of her holdings. Her majordomos tend toward the stodgy. She likes to think she's innovative. After all, she does have a masters in business, and she's very intelligent. Make no mistake about that."

"She hides it very well."

Michael flashed her a grin. "People, especially other

women, tend to discount any good sense Syn might have."

"Out of jealousy."

"Out of prejudice. That young, that beautiful, how could she be smart, as well? It's hardly fair."

"It doesn't happen often."

Michael covered her hand briefly with his. "It's been my good fortune to chance upon such women more than most."

"You're very slippery."

"Syn is also notoriously fickle." Michael blew on his tea and sipped it. "The society pages constantly pair her up with rock stars, athletes and movie stars."

"And video game designers?"

"I can assure you that I have never been in the society pages." He shrugged. "She's concerned mostly with herself, which is what surprises me about her having any kind of relationship with Simon Wineguard."

"Not her type?"

"Syn isn't looking for a father figure and she isn't famous for her charity. Simon doesn't move in her circles."

Molly considered that. "Then why is he staying on her boat?"

"Why don't you ask her?"

"Maybe I will. We're going to be working on this documentary for the next month. If Syn Roderick is going to play a part in managing Simon's time, I'll need to know what I'm dealing with."

"All right, but I'll warn you now that she may simply disappear tomorrow of her own volition." Michael took a small notebook and digital camera from his jacket pocket. "As for the fruits of my research today, it's my considered opinion that Bartholomew Sterling is not a nice chap."

Molly lifted her eyebrows and waited.

"Evidently Simon is likely correct in that Sterling is associated with organized crime." His gaze flicked over his notes.

Though her husband had committed most of the information to memory—he had a steel trap for a mind—he used the notes to keep his presentation organized.

"The man muddles in a lot of things, but he hasn't yet gotten caught in anything his solicitors couldn't get him out of. Or that he hasn't had a fall guy for."

"What connection does he have to the train robbery?"

Michael shrugged. "Other than his young cousin's unfortunate death when the train was wrecked, I haven't found anything."

"Did the Sterling family lose more than Chloe Sterling?"

"Definitely." Michael flipped a few pages and found what he was looking for. "Several paintings from the Sterling collection were stolen in the robbery. Evidently the family had been collectors for generations."

"Bankability. Even in tough economies, art remains almost unaffected by market fluctuations."

"Whoever the robbers were, they got away with millions of pounds when they disappeared."

The waitress arrived with their plates and served them. After replenishing their drinks, she quickly left.

Michael tucked into his food and ate with a hearty appetite. Molly watched him and wondered again what kind of boy he had been. Seeing his pure enthusiasm for his food, she felt certain the distance between adult and child bridged easily.

A shadow suddenly fell over her, blotting out the sun and bringing a slight chill.

"Excuse me." The voice sounded like it came from the deep hollows of a cave.

Glancing up, Molly saw a large man standing behind her chair. Across from her, Michael pushed himself to his feet. His face was hard, all humor gone. A step brought him to Molly's side.

The man must have been nearly six and a half feet tall and was broad and heavy-set. He looked like a weight lifter or a professional boxer. Molly opted for boxer because his nose had obviously been broken a number of times. Despite his build, his suit fit him well. His blond hair was short and neat and his face was vaguely childlike. His eyes, though, were chipped flint.

"Something I can do for you, mate?" Michael spoke calmly, but Molly sensed the tension in him.

The big man smiled, showing gapped front teeth. "Didn't mean to interrupt, Mr. Graham. I was hoping to have a word with you and your lovely wife."

The other patrons were watching them closely. Molly scanned the patio for her police escort and realized the constables had remained parked below. They couldn't see what was happening.

"I don't know you, mate." Michael's gaze never turned away from the man.

"Conway." He didn't offer a hand and faced Michael squarely. "Hershel Conway."

"What can I do for you, Mr. Conway?"

"My employer wishes to talk to you when you have some free time." Conway extended a large hand, a business card dwarfed within it. "He said you can call day or night."

Without glancing at the card, Michael plucked it from the man's big hand. "We're busy at the moment. I can't promise anything."

Conway grimaced, looked like he was going to say something, then shrugged. "Mr. Sterling thought meeting with your wife—with both of you—might prove beneficial. Mutual interests. That sort of thing."

"We'd prefer to get back to our meal now." Michael spoke levelly.

Conway's jaw muscles flexed as if he were swallowing something unpleasant. "Sure. You have a fine day, Mr. Graham. You, too, Mrs. Graham." He turned like a large automaton and lumbered away.

After Conway had disappeared inside the restaurant, Michael sat back down. A bleak expression pulled at his features.

"Lovely."

Molly leaned forward and reached for the business card her husband held. "He did say *Sterling*."

"Yes."

Bartholomew Sterling's business card was cluttered with information regarding investments and various enterprises. A mobile number was scrawled on the reverse.

"You're getting popular, love." Michael pushed his unfinished plate away. "With all the wrong people."

CHAPTER FOURTEEN

EARLY MONDAY MORNING, SIMON Wineguard showed up at the Blackpool Rail Station to start principal shooting for the documentary. His eyes were bleary and he looked hungover. His voice was a gruff roar that carried through the fog-shrouded forest.

Molly rested against her Mini and watched. She hated the standing around. For her it was more fun and challenging to gather facts and write up the grant proposal than to manage the project afterwards. Normally she would have let someone else handle the day-to-day operations and only taken meetings when necessary. Her expertise was dreaming up ways to get monies and people together to support an idea or project. She liked working independently.

The rail station lay just to the west of Blackpool. It had been an afterthought in the late nineteenth century and hadn't made it much past the 1970s. Faded and graffiti-covered band posters fluttered on the station walls.

The actual train robbery had taken place a couple miles away, but Simon had wanted to do some of the preliminary narrative intros in front of a rail station. The video team had cleaned off the front of the building and made it presentable.

The young woman Simon had chosen to provide the narration was dressed warmly against the morning chill, but in the thin sunlight piercing the overhanging tree canopy she looked stark and vulnerable. She'd memorized all her lines and spoke clearly without fault even when Simon made her stop and start over to add emphasis.

A police car rolled up beside Molly's and came to a halt. Inspector Paddington opened the door and climbed out from behind the wheel. He lit his pipe and joined Molly.

"Good morning, Mrs. Graham."

"Good morning, Inspector. What brings you to see us today?"

"Don't worry. I'm not here to bother your director. I came to talk to you."

"All right. I appreciate you keeping the media away from the area."

Only a few BBC reporters and channel news types remained. Since there had been no break in the murder investigation, and nothing substantial to tie the woman's death to the potential missing treasure from the train wreck, most of the media outlets had found other stories to move on to.

Simon broke the narration once more and moved the video crews, then had the young woman begin her spiel again.

"Heard you had a visitor on Saturday." Paddington lit his pipe.

"Actually, I dealt with several. Your two constables should have kept you informed. Was there a particular one you were interested in?"

"Big bloke at the Smokehouse. Fotherby spotted him. Followed him to Grimsby's."

Charlotte Grimsby ran another of the bed-and-breakfasts in Blackpool. The Bullock and Rooster tended toward a lower-rent crowd, usually university students out for a run at the local girls over summer break.

"With as much surveillance as your department is doing on me of late, I'm surprised your constables have time to follow anyone else."

"Fotherby didn't like the way this bloke looked. After I saw him, I liked him even less."

"You drove out here to tell me that?"

Paddington studied her. "I'm concerned about you, Mrs. Graham. Your little production has dipped into some dark places."

"Not counting Mrs. Whiteshire's death?"

"I would never discount that." Paddington frowned. "Did that man say who he works for?"

"He did. Bartholomew Sterling."

"What do you know about Sterling?"

"That he's not an especially nice man."

Paddington spat on the ground and mumbled a curse. "He's a dirty sod is what he is. London Metro has tried to make him for a dozen crimes and can't get anything to stick."

"I'd heard that."

"What did he want with you?"

"To deliver his employer's business card."

"Sterling wants to meet with you?"

"Yes."

Paddington waited, then realized she wasn't going to offer any more information. He sighed. "Well? Have you spoken with him?"

"Wouldn't your constables have mentioned it?"

"We're not monitoring your phone or Internet."

"I'm glad we have some privacy left. Regarding your question, I haven't called Sterling. Michael and I have… reservations about contacting him."

"That's both fortunate and disappointing." Paddington leaned a hip against Molly's little car, which sagged under his weight. "It's fortunate because you don't need to be around his sort. But it's disappointing because you don't know what he wants."

Molly silently agreed. She and Michael had talked about the subject Saturday and Sunday. But they'd decided that it was safer to avoid the man.

"I can't see what he would want with me."

For a moment, Paddington smoked his pipe, seemingly lost in thought. "It might not be you that Sterling's ultimately interested in."

Molly focused on the inspector. "Do you have something to tell me?"

"No." Paddington sighed. "But I feel I *must* tell you. You'll probably find out soon enough." He nodded at Simon Wineguard. "There's no love lost between your director and Sterling."

"I'd heard that, but I don't understand why."

"Simon Wineguard had a daughter. Twenty years old and attending university in London. She was found dead of an overdose six years ago. The investigators on the case didn't find any evidence of foul play, but the girl often frequented one of Sterling's clubs. He has a string of them, actually, and many cater to the younger set. Wineguard pushed the case, urged us to dig for some evidence that could tie his daughter's death to Sterling, but that didn't happen."

"A daughter? Why don't I know anything about her? She didn't show up in the information I read on Simon when I was considering him for the job."

"She went by her mother's name. The story barely touched the papers, but a mate of mine worked the case."

Standing there in the wispy fog, Molly felt colder. She turned up the collar of her long coat. "I'd heard Simon took this project on because he planned to leverage it into a piece on Bartholomew Sterling."

"Any chance of that happening?"

Molly shrugged. "Evidently Simon believes so. One

thing's for certain—he's gotten Bartholomew Sterling's attention."

"I wasn't sure how much of this you were aware of, Mrs. Graham. I thought about going to your husband first, informing him of how dangerous this could potentially be in the hopes that he would talk to you and maybe get you to back away from this project."

"That wouldn't happen, Inspector. Michael might voice his concerns, but he wouldn't try to tell me what to do. Nor would I try to coerce him."

"I figured as much, Mrs. Graham. That's why I came directly to you." Paddington spoke plainly, completely confident in the way he'd handled things. "Still, I wanted you to know you might be at the center of a cross fire. If you didn't know that already."

"I didn't. I appreciate your concern." Molly regarded him. "So what are your plans in light of this?"

For a moment, Paddington just smoked quietly. "I'm going to see what happens. I've still got a murder to investigate. Wouldn't make much sense for me to chase off the principle persons of interest, would it?"

"I suppose not. Have you explored the possibility that Sterling had something to do with Mrs. Whiteshire's death?"

"Some might take it as a warning to Wineguard."

"If Sterling was willing to kill someone, why not go directly after Simon?" Molly couldn't believe she was talking so calmly of murder.

"That's my major argument for not believing Sterling was connected to the murder." Paddington narrowed his eyes. "On the other hand, Simon Wineguard has an equally compelling agenda he's following."

"You already implied that Simon had a motive—publicity."

"Ah, but as you pointed out, now he has another one—he's hoping to leverage this documentary into revenge on Bartholomew Sterling."

"But to kill someone who was not even involved?"

"I suspect Wineguard would be a lot harder to kill than Mrs. Whiteshire. God rest her." Paddington nodded at Simon. "When I questioned him, I recognized a desperate man if I've ever seen one, Mrs. Graham. Near the end of his tether, he is."

Watching Simon yell at the actress and film crew, and remembering how he'd behaved around Syn Roderick, Molly silently agreed. The director wasn't acting like the man she'd interviewed for the documentary months ago.

"And if it wasn't him, perhaps I should take a closer look at that personal assistant of his," Paddington added.

"Miss Abernathy?" That made even less sense than suspecting Simon. "She wouldn't harm a fly."

"Are you sure of that?"

Molly refrained from speaking.

Paddington continued, "Miss Abernathy has got very strong feelings for Mr. Wineguard. That bloke is either a blockhead and doesn't know it, or he chooses to ignore her. Perhaps she thought murdering Mrs. Whiteshire might help draw more attention to her boss's project." Paddington glanced at the line of reporters scattered behind the police sawhorses set up around the rail station. "Seems to be working, if that's the case. This little film of yours has a body count now. That's going to be interesting to a lot of people."

"That's ridiculous."

"Is it?" The inspector gave her a dry, mirthless smile. "I've seen people kill each other for a whole lot less, Mrs. Graham. And whoever wanted Mrs. Whiteshire murdered only had to hire someone to have it done. He—or she—didn't have to do it personally. That makes a difference. More easily denied." He paused and tamped his tobacco down in his pipe. "I'm just suggesting you exercise more caution in dealing with these people."

"I appreciate your concern, Inspector."

"You're welcome. And if you discover something I might be interested in, give me a ring, won't you?" Paddington touched his hat and walked away.

Molly stood there and felt more vulnerable than she had only minutes before. She hated the way her mind kept poking and prodding at all the possibilities Paddington had presented her with. But they wouldn't go away.

PEDALING HIS MOUNTAIN BIKE under the noonday sun, Michael followed the old spur of the rail tracks to the site of the train robbery. His muscles were warm and liquid, moving powerfully as he pushed through the forest. He loved the physical challenge of the terrain. Luckily hunters and kids walked the tracks often enough to leave a trail for him. Still, the ride was uneven and rough, and he was beginning to feel the effort.

He finally crested a hill and looked down into the hollow where the train robbery had taken place. Taking his digital camera from his small backpack, he opened up the black-and-white pictures he'd captured from the microfiche files.

Seeing the site in color and three dimension made identification less obvious. But the general contour of the land matched that in the pictures, confirming the location. Michael thought it was odd not to see the overturned train there. As he'd crested the hill, he'd had the inescapable sense that he would.

Locals had long claimed that Blackpool was home to

a number of ghosts—way before Liam McKenna and his sister had set up Other Syde Haunted Tours.

Is that what you came out here for, mate? To see if there were any ghosts lingering? Michael laughed at himself and reached down to the bike frame for his bottle of water. He drank deeply but not long as he didn't want his muscles to tighten up.

But he wasn't quite ready to go down into the hollow, either.

"Having second thoughts about goin' down there, mon?" The voice was melodic, carrying a hint of the Caribbean with a slight British accent.

The man sat on a boulder to one side of the trail. He was of medium height but had an athletic build, broad shouldered and good looking, with dark skin that hid him in the shadows. His hair hung in dreadlocks to his shoulders, tied with colorful bands. A short goatee framed his mouth. His arms rested on his knees, which were almost level with his chin, and he leaned back against a tree, his bike helmet upside down in his hands. He wore a warmup suit with the jacket left open, showing a bright blue tank top beneath.

"I'm having second thoughts, too." The man grinned, his teeth white against his dark face. "I came out here to see the 'scene of the crime,' so to speak, then I thought about having to climb back up that steep incline." He shook his head good-naturedly. "I don't know if I want to see it bad enough."

Michael unfastened his brain bucket and hung it by the chin strap from one of the handles. "Out here by yourself?"

"I am."

"You with the media?"

The man shook his head. "Not me, mon. No way. I

just recently moved to Blackpool. Workin' as a handyman. Carpentry. Bricklayin'. Swampin' boats an' some engine repair where I can get it."

"You sound like a busy man."

"I try to be, but I wouldn't mind bein' busier. It's hard breakin' into the local circles. They don't much care for strangers 'round here."

"No, they don't. Work would be easier to come by in London."

"Probably. But I heard about this place an' wanted to explore it myself."

"You heard about Blackpool?"

"Yeah, mon. Stories my gran'mother told me. One of my ancestors served aboard a pirate ship a long time ago. He's supposed to be buried 'round here somewhere."

"Unfortunate. Blackpool has a tendency to lose graves from what I've heard."

"Especially from back in the day." Pushing himself off the boulder, the man stood and walked over to Michael. "Rohan Wallace." He offered his hand.

"Pleasure to meet you, Mr. Wallace. Michael Graham." Michael felt the strength and heavy calluses in the other man's grip. Rohan Wallace was definitely an outdoorsman and used to hard labor.

"Just call me Rohan. More used to answerin' that than Mr. Wallace." He grinned.

"Call me Michael."

Rohan nodded. "Your wife is the one that set up the movie everyone's talking about, right?"

"That's right."

"Did that woman's death have anythin' to do with the film? If I'm out of line for askin', mon, just say so."

"That's a question everyone's wondering. I don't have an answer for you. I hope not."

"But there's still the chance. I'm not a big believer in coincidences."

"This coming from the man sitting under a tree when I came out here this morning."

Rohan laughed, and the sound was free and easy and musical. "*That* was a coincidence. I didn't even know I was going to be out here today until I found myself here lookin' over that hill. Then I thought I'd sit a bit an' think about it a little more."

Despite Rohan's genial nature, Michael couldn't help but be a tad wary. The last few days had taken some strange turns, and it seemed many people involved in the documentary had misrepresented themselves.

"Just sightseeing?" Michael put his bottle of water back on the bike frame.

Rohan's eyes brightened and he hid them behind a pair of wraparound sunglasses with ruby lenses. "You think I'm out here treasure huntin', mon?"

"A lot of people in Blackpool have taken up the hobby."

"That's true. But if I'd been in the mood for treasure huntin', I'd have stayed in Kingston. Got all kinds of stories about pirate ships down there."

"I suppose you do."

"My gran'mother tells me not to invest in such foolishness. She says a man learns to do things wit' his hands." Rohan held up his callused hands. "That's all the treasure he gets in this world."

"Sounds like your grandmother is a smart lady."

"The smartest, mon." Rohan thrust his chin down at the hollow. "Want to go down? Gonna be a long haul comin' back up."

"Sure." Michael hated the idea of leaving a task unfinished. He climbed on the bike and pushed himself forward.

CHAPTER FIFTEEN

WALKING BETWEEN THE PAST and the present in his mind, Michael laid out the scene the morning the robbers attacked the train. His imagination was so finely attuned with the events that he could almost hear the tortured scream of metal, the frantic hiss of the steam from the overturned and smashed pulling engine, and the panicked cries of the wounded and dying.

"It must have taken the police a long time to get out here." Rohan stood nearby with his hands in his pockets. Much of his lighthearted demeanor had vanished, leaving him a more somber companion.

"Over forty minutes." Michael stepped onto a length of rusting rail track that shifted under his weight. "Some people reported that it was closer to an hour. When all of this happened, it must have been horrible and confusing."

"Somethin' like this usually is. I've seen shipwrecked crews come back to shore freaked out of their heads. Had to help pull some of them out of the sea at times. People in the middle of something like that, even when you're helpin', you don't quite keep it together."

"It would be difficult."

"Didn't they have a radio? Weren't they invented then?"

"They were, but the transmissions were spotty here." Michael looked back up at the tall hill. "Down here, reception was almost nonexistent." He took his iPhone from his pocket and checked the connection bars. He was down to one. Smiling ruefully, he returned the phone to his pocket. "Not a whole lot better now, even with geosynchronous satellites."

"How did the town find out?"

"A fourteen-year-old boy that had hired on as manual labor went for help. He was a Blackpool local picked for the run."

"He knew the area."

Michael walked down the rails and pictured the scene. The boy had to have been terrified. "He did know the area, but he was also lucky. The train robbers spotted him and pursued him for a while. They shot at him several times. His mother was also one of the survivors, and she said she'd lain out here with her daughter thinking that each shot she heard was going to be the death of her son."

"Brave kid."

"Very brave kid."

"What happened to him?"

"Joined up near the end of World War II and was killed fighting the Germans in France."

Rohan grimaced sympathetically. "Tough break."

"Yes, it was." As Michael had dug through the material at the library, he'd thought of all the stories that he could tell. Whenever he encountered something that fascinated him, his mind naturally turned to game play and ways to set up the reveals for the players.

"The robbers knew they had some time to get out of here with the goods," Rohan said as he kept pace with Michael on the other side of the tracks. "But they didn't have all day. They had to move fast."

"But where would they go?"

"It would be easy to disappear in the woods, but that

wouldn't keep someone determined to find them from discoverin' them. An' they would have left tracks."

"Yeah. But these guys…they just disappeared."

Rohan shrugged. "I suppose the roads an' the sea would be the easiest ways to go."

"The military had float planes in the harbor the day of the scheduled delivery." Michael glanced around at the trees and was awed by the ruggedness of the countryside. "They checked the roads and the shore. Autos and boats got pulled over."

"But no art, no gold."

"No."

"Maybe these guys got past security anyway."

"It's possible."

Rohan took a deep breath. "Or the gold an' those paintings are still out here."

Michael shook his head. "The robbers didn't set this heist up to fail. They came for the gold and they got it. Maybe the paintings were a bonus."

"Unless the paintings were what they were after. The gold would have been harder to transfer. But paintings? They'd be light. They could have escaped with the art while everybody was lookin' for the gold."

The thought wasn't new to Michael. He'd been turning it around in his mind, as well. But he was surprised at how easily the notion occurred to Rohan. And then Michael realized he was standing out in the forest a long way from home with someone he really didn't know.

Rohan glanced at him. "How much were those paintings worth?"

"Millions."

"That's a lot of reasons to do this. Then you have to wonder 'bout the people transferrin' those paintings. People in circles like that, they'd talk. Maybe they asked each other if they were willin' to risk moving their artwork. Makes you think how many of them trusted each other." Rohan paused. "An' if there was somebody among them that wasn't worth trustin'."

Michael scratched his chin. He'd already considered that, as well, but he was taken aback how thoroughly Rohan Wallace seemed to have studied the matter. "That's not a scenario that would readily come to everyone."

Rohan shrugged and gave a small laugh. "I'm suspicious of people."

"Any people in particular?"

For a moment, Rohan merely walked on in silence as they followed the tracks. Then he glanced at Michael. "The Crowe family seems to be involved in a number of things that have happened in Blackpool. How involved were they in this shipment?"

Michael knew the answer to that. "The military liaisons set up a temporary command center at Crowe's Nest. At Philip Crowe's invitation. He was the head of the family at the time."

Rohan laughed softly. "I guess that tells you how much information the Crowe family might have had about that shipment, doesn't it?"

"Yes." Michael had already considered that, too.

"You gotta ask yourself if that particular Crowe was any more trustworthy than the rest of the family."

SYN RODERICK MET SIMON Wineguard at the small restaurant inside the Glower Lighthouse. She was dressed in a light green blouse, white Capri pants tailored to show off her figure, and a loose sweater.

Parked across the street, Molly debated going in after them. If she did, she knew they'd notice her immediately. The restaurant didn't seat a lot of people and the intimate environment made anonymity impossible. People went there to see and be seen.

Someone knocked on the passenger window. When she looked to her left, Fred Purnell stood on the curb and waved at her. Molly rolled the window down.

"Hello, Molly. I suppose you followed Simon in from the video shoot."

"I did. And you must have followed Miss Roderick."

Fred grinned. "I did. In from her yacht at the marina. Interesting woman, that one, and I was intrigued by how she fits into all this."

"Old friend of Simon's, I hear."

Fred rolled disbelieving eyes. "Not that one." He nodded at the lighthouse. "You're not going inside?"

"They would assume I was spying."

"Of course. The very reason I chose to remain outside, as well. Because we are." Fred pointed at the passenger seat on her left. "May I sit? I have news about Miss Roderick's relationship with Simon Wineguard you might find fascinating. I thought perhaps we could share."

Molly unlocked the door and the newspaper reporter slid into the seat.

Fred held up a brown paper bag. "I brought tea and scones. Would you care for some?"

"Please." Molly took one of the disposable cups of tea and a scone wrapped in a paper napkin. "At least one of us came prepared for spying."

"Years of training, my dear. You're still new to it. Never fear. You'll soon get the hang of it."

"I hope not. I intend to never get involved in something like this again."

"Spying?"

"Murder."

"Oh. That." Fred grimaced. "Well, that's simply bad luck."

"Worse for Mrs. Whiteshire."

"Quite. I gather you know about Simon Wineguard's daughter?"

"Died in one of Bartholomew Sterling's nightclubs. The inspector dropped by this morning and told me."

"I thought he might. Especially after Sterling's bruiser intercepted you and Michael."

"You seem particularly well-informed." Molly took a bite of the scone.

"I am the best reporter in all of Blackpool, after all." Fred smiled gently. "And I was really good whilst I was in London." He pointed toward the lighthouse. "As to why Miss Roderick is here, she and Wineguard appear to have joined up for a treasure hunt."

That surprised Molly. "They can't possibly believe anything stolen from the train is still in Blackpool."

Fred glanced at her and looked amused. "My dear, Friday night you as much as announced that very thing to the whole town."

"I intimated that."

"Very well, I must say. You had everyone's attention. Many were convinced. I've heard people have been going to the library in droves. Michael must have seen them while he was there poking about."

Molly sipped her tea and gave the possibility some thought. "A treasure hunt." She shook her head dismissively.

"I'm sure you personally researched the train robbery, but is it possible that Simon Wineguard and his people explored the subject further?"

"That was part of his job."

"Are you certain that he shared everything with you that he discovered?"

Thinking back on all the things Simon hadn't told her, Molly immediately felt frustrated. "No."

"My research into Miss Roderick's background indicates that she doesn't always make her money in a legitimate fashion."

"Where did you hear that? Michael knows—knew—her and didn't mention anything of the sort."

"I still have a few friends left on the Metro in London. The inspector I chatted with was as surprised as I was that Miss Roderick had come to Blackpool. He went on to say that lately Miss Roderick has dabbled in blackmail."

"How do you *dabble* in blackmail?"

"Miss Roderick has always been in the public eye. She's used her influence to get close to a few people she later threatened to expose for one thing or another—drugs, sex, insider stocks trading—in order to leverage good positions for herself in various social and economic interests."

Lovely woman you know, Michael. Molly realized that was unfair and felt a wisp of regret, but she was human and a woman like Syn Roderick hit her personal radar as a threat. Focusing, Molly took a breath, sipped her tea and turned the possibilities around in her mind. No matter how she connected them, they didn't turn out well.

"I doubt she's blackmailing Simon."

Fred gazed out the window. The steam from his tea fogged up the glass when he took off the lid. "Nor do I. But their relationship is fascinating, no matter how it works. Because there has to be something at the heart of it."

MICHAEL LOCKED HIS MOUNTAIN bike to a post in front of the Blackpool Café. He was tired from the long ride, and more frustrated by his inability to let go of the mystery of the train robbery than he should have been. The distraction prevented him from noticing Hershel Conway's approach until the man was nearly on top of him.

For a big man, he moves awfully quietly. Tension knotted Michael's stomach as he straightened up to face the man. He let the bike helmet dangle by its chin strap from his fingers. It wasn't much of a weapon, but at least it was something.

"Mr. Conway. How unexpected."

Rohan Wallace stood by his bike only a few feet away. They'd agreed to get a pint.

"This mon a friend of yours, Michael?" With a casual step, Rohan moved in beside Michael.

"New acquaintance, actually." Michael never took his gaze from Conway. "We're still getting to know each other. He's insistent."

"Mr. Graham, my employer would like a moment with you." Conway jerked a thumb over a massive shoulder toward a gunmetal-gray sedan parked across the street. "Since you and the missus declined Mr. Sterling's invitation, he thought he'd come to you."

"I'm surprised he was able to find me."

"Serendipity. We'd just finished dining here and were about to leave when you and your friend pulled up."

"This is still an inconvenient time, I'm afraid."

Conway breathed in and out like a stymied bull. "Let's be frank, Mr. Graham, Mr. Sterling would like very much to talk to you. He's stayed away from your wife because he thought you would take exception to that. He's gone out of his way to respect you. He could have gone to speak with her this morning at the video shoot. He's trying to go through...proper channels. Man to man."

A chill ghosted through Michael and his mouth went dry.

"Don't know about you, Michael, but that sounds like

a threat to me." Rohan's voice became deadly calm and he focused on Conway. "Maybe you and I should see how high this guys bounces."

Conway pulled his coat away enough to reveal the pistol tucked into a holster on his waistband. He grinned broadly, but there was no humor in his expression. "I don't *bounce* so easily." He never took his eyes from Michael. "And I'm not a patient man. I think we should all be civilized and allow Mr. Sterling to go inside and buy you a drink. How does that sound?"

"Like I don't have much of a choice," Michael replied.

"I told Mr. Sterling that you were a bright lad."

CHAPTER SIXTEEN

BARTHOLOMEW STERLING WORE a dark blue double-breasted suit that fit his squared-off frame and added a little height. Silver rose-shaped cufflinks gleamed at his coat sleeves. Michael figured the man was five feet six inches tall in lifts. Carefully coiffed gray-blond hair hung down over his forehead and gave him a carefree appearance. He looked like a university fop gone to seed in his mid-fifties.

The Blackpool Café catered to the blue-collar crowd but attracted a lot of families and young people who passed through the town on holiday or on a leg of their sailing jaunt. Lobster nets hung across the ceiling, holding starfish, mollusk shells and driftwood.

"Let's sit here." Sterling waved toward a dark booth near the front entrance. He glanced at Rohan Wallace, who had walked into the restaurant with Michael. "I'll be happy to set your friend up with a drink, but I'm afraid this is for your ears only."

Rohan glanced at Michael, who nodded.

"I'm gonna be at the bar. In case you need something."

"Thanks, mate."

With a last glance at Conway, Rohan strode to the bar and sat where he could keep them within easy view.

Michael slid into the booth and was immediately trapped by Conway's bulk as the big man maneuvered in beside him. He glanced at Conway. "You realize that if you try anything…"

"That your friend is going to stop me?" Conway grinned at Rohan and shook his head, looking like an evil child. "Not on his best day."

"I was going to say that he'd call the police."

"I've seen the police. Got to say, I'm not impressed."

Moving carefully, Sterling sat opposite them in the booth. "Well, Mr. Conway, we don't want the police involved in our business."

"Yes, sir." Conway's menace dialed down a kilowatt or two.

"I want to assure you, Mr. Graham, that I wish you no harm." Sterling smiled disarmingly. It was a smile that showed practiced ease and Michael was certain it worked on a lot of people. "I'm only here to rectify an old injustice in whatever way I'm able. Not to threaten you in any way."

"Unfortunately, the circumstances—and present company—don't allow for that."

"I'm going to work to ameliorate the situation, hopefully."

A young waitress arrived and Sterling ordered pints all around, as well as one for Rohan at the bar. Sterling remained affable and unruffled, and even flirted slightly with the young woman.

Michael waited and tried to keep from panicking. It was one thing to react to sudden danger and another to sit in the middle of it. Still, he was surprised to find that he was calmer than he probably ought to have been under the circumstances.

"I wanted to talk to you about the train robbery, Mr. Graham." Sterling dragged a forefinger around the rim of his glass. "Do you know all the people that were involved?"

"I made a list of all those noted."

"My uncle was one of them."

Michael nodded. "I've seen his name."

"He lost more than the paintings that were aboard that train."

"His daughter."

"My cousin, yes." Sterling's head dipped in acknowledgment. "But even more than that. Do you know why those men were shipping their art acquisitions out of London, Mr. Graham?"

"To keep them safe. The Nazis were bombing the city almost daily."

"Are you an art collector?"

"Not so much. Molly and I pick up a few pieces now and again." Mostly they were from artists Michael worked with on his video games.

"Why do you make those purchases?"

Michael hesitated, trying to figure out where Sterling was going with his line of questioning. "Because we see something we like. Or we're on holiday and want a piece to remember the trip."

Leaning forward a little, Sterling held Michael's gaze. "A great many people buy paintings for those very reasons. But they usually don't spend large sums of money. They want paintings they can hang in their homes or offices so that others can appreciate the same beauty, or their good taste and wealth. You understand?"

"Of course."

"Not everyone buys paintings for those reasons. Many collectors purchase art for investment purposes only. Art is unique. One of a kind. As such, the intrinsic value of a piece, or a painter, rarely gets hit by economic fluctuations even in the hardest of times." Sterling sipped his pint. "Most of the men who placed collections aboard that ill-fated train were that kind of collector."

"Investors?" That was something Michael hadn't considered.

"Exactly." Sterling touched his nose knowingly and smiled. "You see what I'm driving at?"

"Quite frankly, no. They were trying to safeguard their investments—"

Sterling waved a hand to interrupt. "Why ship those paintings from London? Men like that, they would want to watch over their investments. Especially if they had large sums of their wealth tied up there. And many of them did."

"I still fail to see your point."

Shaking his head, Sterling sighed. "If you have something very valuable, Mr. Graham, what do you do to make certain you don't lose your investment?"

Michael figured out where the man was going. "You would insure them."

"Precisely. Which is what those men did. But, if the paintings were destroyed in the war…" Sterling let the thought hang.

"Insurance wouldn't cover it."

"You grasp the problem."

Michael leaned back in the booth. He wasn't as fearful now as new thoughts consumed his mind. "Insurance companies would pay off on stolen paintings."

"And they did. But the agencies held up the checks for some time. There was a suspicion that German agents intercepted the train." Sterling grimaced. "Years dragged on before the claims were finally settled. Not everyone was happy." Sterling paused and lifted a cautious eyebrow.

"Moreover, claims couldn't be filed on some missing pieces."

"Why?"

"Come, come, Mr. Graham. An intelligent man such as yourself? Why do you think that would happen?"

Michael only had to ponder for an instant before he arrived at an answer. "Ownership could be contested because they had purchased stolen art."

Sterling chuckled, then drank from his pint. His eyes sparkled in merriment. "That was the rub for a few of the men who owned paintings on that train. Hundreds of thousands of investment dollars disappeared in that train sabotage." He paused. "Many of those men, my father and uncle included, believed the mastermind behind the train robbery came from within their circle."

"Someone in the group took advantage of the situation?"

"Yes."

"I don't suppose they knew who to blame?"

"They blamed someone, but there was never any evidence." Sterling shook his head. "My father and uncle wished to pursue the matter. My cousin died aboard that train, one of several who lost their lives. My uncle wanted someone to pay for her death. But there was a war on, and murder and robbery took a backseat to bombings and mass destruction in the streets."

"Given the conditions, that's understandable."

"But it shouldn't have been forgiven."

"I'm not condoning the actions at the time. That was just a statement of fact." Michael was slightly mortified that he'd brushed those deaths off so casually.

"I understand, Mr. Graham." Sterling lowered his voice and tried to sound more relaxed. "I, of course, didn't know my cousin because I was born late in life to my father, but I am appalled that the death of a child has gone unpunished."

"Seventy years." Michael shook his head. "Whoever was behind the train robbery, they're dead and gone now, Mr. Sterling."

"I'm aware of that, but unmasking Chloe's killer can still be beneficial to all. Those paintings—the ones that were undeclared for various reasons—can possibly be recovered by naming those responsible for the robbery."

"How?"

Sterling spoke more softly. "Money usually stays with a family, Mr. Graham. I know that you are new to it, but wealthy families tend to collect it. When managed properly, it snowballs and grows within that family. Nearly all of the men involved in the train robbery have left families who are still wealthy. If I was able to discover, and *prove* indisputably, who arranged that robbery, I would have the means to demand that wealth back."

"You're talking about blackmail."

Sterling waved offhandedly. "You say that as though it's a bad thing, Mr. Graham. In actuality, blackmail is often the price of doing business. Provided one's business isn't on the up and up."

And you would know that firsthand, wouldn't you? Michael took a swallow from his pint to give himself time to think. His thoughts effortlessly formed various constructions and probabilities. This was very much like a game scenario. The problem lay in how best to finesse it.

"Do you have someone in mind, Mr. Sterling?"

With an unctuous smile, Sterling nodded. "Of course I do. The robbery took place within a few miles of here. And the transportation was arranged through a local contact the military department had engaged."

"Philip Crowe."

"Bravo, Mr. Graham." Sterling smiled more broadly and nodded as though he were a proud father. "You're apparently on top of things, and this evidently isn't a new angle for you."

"The possibility had occurred to me." It also explained why Aleister Crowe was so insistent on involving himself in the documentary. Crowe would want to keep the family name from being dragged through the mud.

"As that possibility occurred to my father and uncle."

"Surely they followed up with an investigation."

"They did. But it came to naught."

"Why would something come to light now?"

Sterling leaned back and shook his head. "Nothing may, Mr. Graham, but I'm not predisposed to give up on this since the robbery is once more at the forefront of the media. I doubt there will be a better chance to uncover the truth of the villainy that transpired during that robbery. But we must try, mustn't we?"

"Frankly, I don't see how I can help you."

"We have a commonality that binds us. We can be useful to each other in our separate enquiries. I'm also assured that you're an intelligent man. Quite the puzzle solver, from what I've been told. Moreover, you're part of Blackpool but you still have an outsider's eyes." Sterling pointed to his own eyes. "That is very important when sorting through something like this that is so close to home."

"I think you're misjudging what I can do for you in this matter."

Sterling smiled. "Perhaps. And if I have misjudged you and end up being in any way disappointed, I will claim no foul. You are the best champion I could have in this endeavor, Mr. Graham. After all, a lot of innocent families were injured by this crime. They could stand to benefit when the truth comes out. I only propose a partnership—both of us seeking the truth as to what degree Philip Crowe was involved in the robbery. If that suits you, and if I may be of use in any way, please don't hesitate to call me." He reached into his jacket pocket and took out a white-gold case. He popped the case open and removed a jade-green business card and presented it with a flourish.

The card held only a mobile number.

"You can reach me at that number twenty-four hours a day."

Reluctantly, Michael closed his hand over the card.

After finishing his pint, Sterling stood and Conway left money on the table.

"Good hunting, Mr. Graham. It was a pleasure meeting you."

Michael merely nodded, not knowing what to say. He couldn't bring himself to thank the man for holding him under duress.

Sterling, followed by Conway, left without a backward glance. After they'd gone, Rohan brought his pint over and sat down.

"You okay, mon?"

"Yes." Michael rubbed his chin. "Thanks for hanging about. You could have stepped into a lot of trouble by doing that."

Rohan smiled. "I've always found it's better if you see trouble coming." He stared through the window as the luxury car pulled away from the curb. "This about that robbery?"

"It is."

"Seems like a very dangerous mon."

"That he is." Michael sighed and wondered how deep he was now in with Bartholomew Sterling.

CHAPTER SEVENTEEN

"STOLEN PAINTINGS THAT WERE already stolen? That's what Sterling is here for?" Molly stared at Michael as they sat in front of the fireplace in the den. He had laid a small fire and it was just warm enough to make her feel toasty where she sat curled up on one of the couches.

"Seems a bit insidious, doesn't it?" Michael smiled in that crooked-mouthed fashion he had when he wasn't at all terribly amused. "Sort of like a lethal game of duck, duck, goose. You stole the paintings, he stole the paintings."

"Someone stole the stolen paintings." Molly sipped her wine.

"Exactly."

The room was large and filled with windows along the back wall. It faced the same view as their bedroom above—out to sea in the dark night. Running lights from a few boats passed near the coastline and farther out in deep water. Molly loved turning the lights down low in that room, or having only the fireplace burning, and gazing out the window. With the stars above and the sea below, the sight was magical, as if anything might happen.

She looked at Michael. He sat on the floor in front of the fireplace clad only in lounging pants and a tank top. Furrows cut across his forehead.

Knowing he was frustrated, Molly felt sorry for him. "What are you going to do?"

He glanced up at her, having to pause for a moment as he drew his thoughts back to her. "About what?"

"Bartholomew Sterling."

"You're assuming I might actually stumble onto something to tell the man." Michael joined her on the couch and wrapped his arms around her.

Molly snuggled into him, smelling his soapy fresh scent from the shower. The heat of his chest warmed her. "You might. You're intelligent and resourceful."

Michael kissed her neck and she shivered. "I think I'd rather the whole documentary was dropped and we simply stepped away from this thing," he said. He tried to kiss her again.

Twisting slightly, Molly caught his face against the palm of her hand and stopped him.

"Ouch." Michael leaned back and wiggled his nose experimentally.

"You did not just say that, Michael Graham. Not after all the work and effort I put into this project. Especially since the story is worth telling."

Michael frowned at her. "You have to admit, this documentary has gone wildly astray from where you planned it would."

"Not entirely. I had hoped that some of those secrets buried seventy years ago would come out. But if they hadn't, the story of those displaced people would have been good. There's a lot of displaced people in the world these days. I thought perhaps Blackpool's tale might draw attention to some of the recent problems and win support for them."

"I know, love. It's just that I'm at a loss as to what to do."

"We keep on doing what we're doing, of course. I work

on the documentary, and you return to your game. But you didn't answer my question about Sterling."

"For now all I have planned is to research the paintings a little more. See if I can find out anything about the ones that went missing."

"The police did that already."

"That was back then. There was a war on, and they didn't have the Internet." Michael stared into her eyes. "What's your next step? Despite what you said I have a suspicion it has as much to do with your official job as mine."

She smiled. "Try to figure out what the burglars were looking for when they broke into Mrs. Whiteshire's home and ours."

"All with Paddington's blessing?"

Molly shrugged. "Not exactly. But apparently he's not beating the bushes at the moment, is he?"

"I think the inspector is more concerned about containing a potential situation than in creating one. And there are a number of powerful people involved in this."

"Do you think that impresses him?"

"No, but powerful people always have powerful barristers. Once a suspect gets behind a legal barricade, they're harder to get to."

"You think Paddington's working on this, Michael?"

"I do. Do you know what else I think?"

Molly looked up at him. "What?"

"I think you've talked about this enough tonight." Without another word, Michael scooped her up in his arms and laid her in front of the fireplace.

STRIDING INTO THE BREAKERS, one of Blackpool's upscale dining establishments, Molly waved off the maître d' and strode straight for Aleister Crowe's table. He sat in the middle of his meal, his notebook computer open in front of him, an earbud in one ear hooked to his mobile, and a men's fashion catalogue open beside the computer.

At the last minute, Crowe spotted Molly approaching and disconnected from both computer and mobile. By the time she reached him, he stood tall, calm and collected, elegant in his suit. She disliked the fact that he could keep his aplomb so readily.

"Mrs. Graham. What a pleasant surprise." He blotted his lips with his napkin.

"Can we talk?"

"Perhaps a cup of tea?" Crowe waved over a server. Ever the gentleman, he pulled out Molly's chair.

Molly thanked him, irritated that she hadn't pulled out her own chair before he could get to it, and sat. The server waited on her expectantly. "A glass of water, please."

Crowe sat and removed his computer from the table. He looked at Molly quizzically.

Molly searched his dark eyes and couldn't help sensing again that the man had depths to him that she'd never seen. Darkness seemed to cling to Aleister Crowe. Molly focused on why she was here. "This documentary is causing a lot of talk and speculation. As it turns out, some of it concerns the train robbery itself."

"What speculation would that be?"

"That the train robbery was an inside job, planned by someone who was also part of the planning of Operation Pied Piper."

Crowe shook his head in dismay. "Of course it was. There was some suspicion that government employees were behind it. Possibly military personnel. And there were even a few who believed Hitler and his generals had deciphered information regarding the train shipment and had intercepted it. To fund the Nazi war effort."

"Or that one of the individuals who owned art being shipped on that train masterminded the whole operation to acquire the other paintings."

A grin spread across Crowe's thin lips. "Naturally, since my grandfather allowed the army to set up a command center in my home for the exodus of women and children from London, my family is suspect." He blotted his lips a final time, then put his napkin in the center of his plate. "As to your thinly veiled accusation, I refute any suggestion that my family was responsible for the theft of the paintings or the gold bullion from that train. Will there be anything else? I, for one, am busy and don't have time for idle chitchat." Crowe opened his computer and placed it back on the table.

"Not at the moment." As gracefully as she could, Molly got to her feet.

"I should tell you one thing further, Mrs. Graham." Crowe glared at her through slitted eyes. "If you by any chance allow this rootless speculation to air in your documentary, I will sue all concerned—including you—for libel."

"Mr. Crowe, everything that goes into that documentary will be fact. I assure you of that." Molly held his gaze without batting an eye. "And if I find any proof of culpability on the part of your family, I'll hang it out there for all to see. Just like I will anything else." She turned on her heel and left.

Outside the restaurant, Molly was surprised to find how rapidly her heart was beating. Aleister Crowe was different from any man she'd ever known. He was creepy. And dangerous. There was something cold and chilling about him that she couldn't quite put her finger on.

Or maybe you just don't want to.

Molly took a deep breath and let herself into her Mini

Cooper. She'd just turned the engine over when her mobile rang. The Caller ID read Private Number.

"Hello."

"Mrs. Graham? This is Synthia Roderick. I was with Simon Wineguard the other morning."

"Hello, Miss Roderick."

"I was hoping maybe we could chat."

"All right." In fact, Molly had meant to approach the woman herself that afternoon.

"Excellent. Would you care to meet somewhere? Or would you mind dropping by the boat? I tend to gather a crowd when I go somewhere."

So does a cow pie. "The boat will be fine. What time?"

"Now would be perfect. If you are available."

"I am."

"Brill. I'll see you in a few." Syn rang off without another word.

CHAPTER EIGHTEEN

"Why is it when you think of bloody criminals you call me, mate?"

Michael laughed as he put his friend on speakerphone and carried a cup of tea over to the window of his home office and peered out. "Because you're the only criminal I know, Keith."

"I'm not a criminal." His friend and illustrator feigned a hurt tone.

"Since your definition of criminal only includes people who have been apprehended while breaking the law and police suspicion counts for nothing, I'll agree with you. However, I think *you'll* agree that you do have far more experience with unsavory types than I do."

"Not true. I have not once pandered to the Los Angeles video game producers or Silicon Valley types. I am only a lowly artist—"

"Of no mean skill who has a somewhat checkered past."

"I prefer *colorful.*"

"Whatever."

Keith gave a sigh long enough to travel the entire distance from London to Blackpool. Before breaking into video game design, he'd lived on the street and by his wits, staying one step ahead of police inspectors trying to ferret him out.

He had also had a hand-to-mouth career in advertising,

comics and portrait sitting. When he'd gotten in with Michael, Keith was considering having to go into criminal activity full-time to support his mother.

"Look, mate." Michael kept his voice soft and easy. "I know this is a sore point with you, and I wouldn't bring it up if it weren't necessary. We—Mol and I—are in a bit of a sticky wicket out here."

"In Blackpool?" Keith sounded incredulous. "Mate, there's nothing out there."

"We have ghosts."

"You don't believe in ghosts."

"Doesn't mean they're not real, mate."

Keith laughed and cursed. "You get me up early for this?"

"You should already be in the studio revising those mermaids."

"I mean, I can't believe you took me away from my work."

Michael grinned. Keith tended to be a layabout till there was a fire under him. He was at his best whenever a deadline loomed.

"Have you been watching the news?"

"No. Not since I got my new UFC DVDs in the post." Keith was a consummate fan of the Ultimate Fighting Championship.

"There is a real world out there, mate."

"You and I don't make any money in that world, Michael. We thrive on fantasy and other people's experiences so we can come up with our own."

"True." Michael looked back at his office. Books, comics and action figures filled all the available space. Posters of superheroes and movies covered the walls. A stack of nonfiction books on mythology, history, art and science fought for space with magazines on the same topics. Anything to help fuel his imagination.

"What do you need, Michael? Whatever it is, I'd never leave you in the lurch, no matter how loath I was to do something."

That was precisely why Michael had called. "You had an uncle that was an art forger."

"Uncle Morrie. Sure. My mother's brother."

"Is he still around?"

"If by *around* you mean on this side of the dirt, sure. But he's in the clink again. Pulling three to five this time for forgery. His hand's just not as sure these days. I tell him that, but he doesn't listen to me."

"I thought you had him set up with an advertising agency."

"I did. His hand's fine for that. He was making a decent wage there."

"What happened?"

"Got into some bookies pretty deeply. Didn't utter a word to me. Even if he had, I couldn't have helped him. Uncle Morrie never stops self destructing till he's way past his eyeballs. Guys who busted him for forgery? They were the bookies he owed. They turned on him when he palmed a bad painting off on them. He's lucky they left him breathing." Keith blew out a breath himself. "Truth to tell, Uncle Morrie's probably better off inside than out. He gets meals, dental and a physician's care while he's there. Out here, he don't take care of himself so well. Mum worries about him, and that's not good for her."

"Can you talk to him?"

"I do every week. Take him a carton of ciggies to trade out with the other inmates so he can get what he needs." Keith laughed. "Uncle Morrie's got quite the prison tat business going inside. Getting to be a real *artiste*. The ciggies go toward buying ink and needles, which are contraband inside."

Michael sat at his desk and turned on the monitor. On-screen, several reproductions of paintings stood in neat rows. The images were all of art that had gone missing from the train robbery. Most were in black and white, but they were clear enough that the details could be made out.

"Why are you asking about Uncle Morrie?"

"I need some information about an art theft that happened back in 1940."

"Mate, that's not gonna happen. Uncle Morrie is old, but he isn't that old. I swear, it wasn't him. Besides that, he's an artist, not a booster."

"I thought maybe he could ask around, see if anyone knows something."

"If a mate was involved, Michael, Uncle Morrie's not gonna grass on him. He's never been that kind of bloke."

"I wouldn't ask, but I don't have a lot of places I can go."

"Well, I can send it up the flagpole, mate. Don't know if you'll get anything from him, but I can try."

"I appreciate it, Keith. Will you be able to talk to him soon?"

"If it's that important, I can go today. Now that I'm up…away from my work, I mean. But it's gonna cost you a carton of ciggies."

"All right. Let me e-mail you the information and the paintings I'm interested in. See what Uncle Morrie knows and get back to me." Michael switched off his mobile and glared at the computer screen.

Then he leaned back in his chair and reimagined the scene of the train robbery. If he'd just gotten his hands on gold bullion—*because, mate, if I was bent, there is no bloody way I'm gonna leave that behind!*—how would he get it out of there?

SYN RODERICK WAS PROPERLY dashing in white sailor pants that hugged her every curve, and she knew it. It showed in the smug smile she wore when greeting Molly. The red-and-white striped top molded to Syn's body and left her tanned midriff bare. A sapphire gleamed in her navel and lent her a positively exotic look.

"Molly, so nice to see you again." Syn held out her hand.

Though she didn't want to, Molly took the woman's hand. She also hated that if Syn Roderick's greeting was ersatz, and it had to be, she couldn't detect it.

"Please sit." Syn waved to the small table in the boat's stern. "I thought we could stay out here and enjoy the sea."

"Of course." Molly took a seat under the shade of the festive umbrella. The attendant arrived and Syn asked her for a martini and Molly requested a Diet Coke.

"Since we have a common interest, I thought it might be best if we got this matter sorted." Syn curled her legs underneath herself in her chair and managed to appear elfin and innocent.

Molly couldn't help thinking that the woman reminded her a lot of the jealous queen that gave the poisoned apple to Sleeping Beauty. Guiltlessly, she rather liked the thought and believed she would hang on to it.

Syn tapped her glass with her fingernails. "Okay, let's start with why Simon wished to do this documentary."

"At first I believed he wanted to do the story because it was a good one. I now realize that's not true."

Syn smiled a little. "You know about his daughter?"

"Yes. Her death must have been hard."

"It was." Syn stared into the contents of her glass. "She was my friend at university. Did anyone tell you that?"

"No." The pain in the young woman's eyes looked real to Molly. "I'm sorry for your loss."

"It was a bigger loss than you might assume. Jenna was my only friend." Syn drained her glass and the attendant whisked it away without a word. "My only *true* friend. I suppose you've heard something of me."

"I gather tabloids are quite generous when it comes to you."

Syn grimaced. "My main concern is keeping Simon safe."

"From whom?"

"From Aleister Crowe and Bartholomew Sterling. Both of those men are capable of using violence to get what they want. The death of that woman should have told you that."

"We can't be sure her death is even linked to the documentary."

"You may not be sure. But I am." Syn leaned back against the chair and lifted her head up like she was queen of the realm. "Simon said that woman was killed because of what she knew."

"What did Mrs. Whiteshire know?"

"Simon hasn't been specific, but he says it would change things between him and Bartholomew Sterling."

"Change them how?"

"By giving him the upper hand. Whatever it is could destroy Sterling's world if he wants it to."

Molly took a breath. "If that's true, as much as Simon hates Sterling, why hasn't he already used it?"

Syn shook her head and her pale locks tousled in controlled disarray for a moment. "I can't answer that." She paused and took another sip. "I also know Philip Crowe planned to steal the paintings aboard the train."

"Can you prove that?"

"No."

"Can Simon?"

"Possibly. As I said, he isn't being very forthcoming. I thought perhaps you could talk to him and get something from him. You also knew the Whiteshire woman, and Simon was interested in her. I figured you might have information I didn't."

"And if I did, that I might share?"

Lifting a shoulder, Syn looked nonchalant. "It would only seem fair."

Molly was still considering how to respond to that when the boat's captain entered the stateroom. Tall and rangy, Hugh Dorrance was dressed in khakis today.

"Miss Roderick, if we're going to make your appointment, we're going to need to get underway."

One of Dorrance's sleeves was raked back and an intricate tattoo stood out on his forearm. The skin art was in black ink and faded in places. Molly thought it was a snake coiled around some kind of rifle, but she couldn't be certain.

Dorrance caught her staring and quickly dragged his cuff down to cover the tattoo.

"Thank you, Captain. I hadn't forgotten, but I hadn't realized it was so late, either." Syn turned her attention back to Molly. "It was a pleasure talking to you. Mostly. I hope you'll find the information I gave you useful. And if you should feel inclined to compare notes, you have my card."

CHAPTER NINETEEN

SEATED IN HER CAR AT THE marina, Molly watched as *Crystal Dancer* powered out toward deeper water. Syn Roderick didn't appear on the deck, and Molly couldn't help feeling that the woman was running from something. At that moment the double bell of her phone call was answered.

"Hello, love," Michael said through her earpiece. He sounded happy.

"That woman is detestable."

"I suppose I don't have to ask whom we're talking about."

"If you do, you're much less intelligent than I thought you were when I married you."

"You think that already."

Despite her mood, Molly smiled at the quip. "You're right."

"So maybe you want to fill me in on what's happened."

Putting the car in gear, Molly backed out of the parking space and sped up the hill leading down to the bay. In the distance, Glower Lighthouse stood guard over its rocky promontory. She quickly relayed the conversation she'd had with Syn Roderick, and threw in the one with Aleister Crowe for good measure.

"So Syn believes that Simon has something he can blackmail Bartholomew Sterling with?" Michael's voice was quiet and steady, and Molly knew that he was thinking through the information.

"So it would seem."

"But why tell you?"

"To put pressure on Simon."

"You're going to put pressure on Simon?"

"Michael, I'm involved in this production. I've promised several people a great many things in return for their help. And their money. I misjudged Simon. I'm not used to doing that."

"I wouldn't be so hard on yourself. Too many things were hidden."

"Still, if the documentary is going to go south, I need to do damage control while I can." Molly took a deep breath. "So of course I'm going to put pressure on Simon. I'll get in touch with Miss Abernathy before I approach him. Then we'll ambush him."

"I called Keith. Asked him to talk to his Uncle Morrie."

Molly had heard many stories about the infamous uncle. "Whatever for?"

"On the off chance that he might know something about the train robbery."

"But if he did, wouldn't he have talked before now?"

"Sure. But maybe the information was ignored back then. Or the police couldn't make the case. Or no one was able to connect the dots. I also contacted the insurance agencies that had to pay off on the stolen art."

"I hadn't thought about that." Molly considered the prospect now. "If any of them are willing to talk, it could put a different spin on the documentary."

"Here's another one for you. Apparently at least a few of the pieces of art that disappeared were forgeries."

"How did you find that out?"

"Followed the paper trail created in the newspapers. You have to love Google. As it happens, one of the pieces that was stolen was a painting called *An Afternoon at the Fair*. It was done by a woman at the Paris Exposition in 1889."

"I've never heard of that work."

"Not surprising. The painting was a modest piece, but because of the gender of the artist and the subject matter—especially with an incomplete Eiffel Tower in the background—it was unique."

"That painting was on the train?"

"Yes. The original owner was Mrs. Reginald Featherstone, now deceased. The insurance agency reimbursed her for the loss, once they couldn't prove German soldiers were responsible for the robbery. However, the work has been sold twice since it was stolen. Once in 1958 and again in 1973."

"I guess that painting is popular."

"Paintings."

Molly paused. "There's more than one?"

"There are at least three. The '58 and '73 paintings were both forgeries. The insurance agency, Bristol and Brinker, Limited, found out about the sales in open auction and discovered they were copies when they went to the sales to claim the paintings as agency assets."

"Because, technically, since they paid off on the claim, the agency owns the original."

"Exactly. Cutting through the red tape and legal problems took a while, but Bristol and Brinker executives evidently carry a chip on their shoulders where the Blackpool Robbery is concerned. That's what they call it—the Blackpool Robbery."

"Lovely."

"Isn't it? In fact, they've got a representative in town."

"Do they?"

"Yes. I'm supposed to meet him in a little while. Want to come along?"

Molly thought about the opportunity, then decided against it. "I have to get my hands on Simon as soon as possible. And before I do that, I want to talk to Miss Abernathy."

"YOU SHOULD REALLY TALK to Simon about this, Mrs. Graham." Miss Abernathy sat in front of her notebook computer in her room at the bed-and-breakfast watching film footage that had been shot over the last few days. She froze frames, cropped out sections, and began again.

The woman looked even worse than before. Her eyes had hollowed out and her complexion was pasty. She had a pot of coffee on the warmer and the aroma filled the room. A small metal ashtray from a pub sat near the computer and was filled to overflowing.

"Simon's my next stop." Molly stood nearby. She hadn't tried to sit down since she'd entered the room. "I wanted to see you first."

"Simon knows more about this project than I do."

"Maybe, but you know *Simon* better than I do. Right now I need your expertise, not his."

The woman sighed and shook her head. "No one's an expert on Simon Wineguard. Not even Simon." She paused, then finally turned away from the computer. Her eyes were red-rimmed, as if she'd been crying. She reached for another cigarette and lit up.

Molly stifled the impulse to tell her that the bed-and-breakfast was nonsmoking. She was certain Miss Abernathy was fully aware of that.

"I wish you had met him before Jenna died." Miss Abernathy breathed out smoke as she spoke. "Simon's divorce from her mother and Jenna's troublesome behavior

slowed him down a little. For a while. But he recovered."
She smiled weakly. "Simon's never been at a loss where
women are concerned. That's why his marriage broke up.
But Jenna's death…well, he took that hard."

"So he blamed Bartholomew Sterling."

"The man is a monster." Miss Abernathy's tone was
crisp, like each word was razor-edged and she had to be
careful getting it out. "He makes his money in drugs, but
no one has ever been able to prove it. Jenna died from badly
cut drugs someone sold to her in one of his clubs. Sterling
allows that kind of business to go on in his places because
he profits from it."

"Synthia Roderick insinuated that Simon has something
on Sterling. Something that he can use against him."

Miss Abernathy shook her head again and flicked ashes
into the ashtray. "You can't trust that woman. She manipu-
lates Simon. Plays him like a violin. And he can't see it."

"She says she was a friend of his daughter's."

"Jenna and Synthia met a few times, that's all. There
was no deep friendship. She likes to tell Simon they were
close, and Simon likes to believe it. But what she's really
after is her own means of blackmailing Sterling. They both
despise him."

"Blackmailing him for what?"

"I assume it has to do with the train robbery." Miss
Abernathy stubbed her cigarette out. "There is one more
thing Simon was holding back from you."

Molly waited.

"He had it on good authority that the robbery was an
inside job. Not only that, but several of the paintings were
forgeries. Some of the people who'd shipped their art figured out a way to turn a profit, as well."

Memory of the forged paintings Michael had mentioned
twisted through Molly's mind. "So the owners of the stolen

art filed claims for their losses with the various insurance agencies and were reimbursed for them, but someone made forgeries so that they could double their money."

"Exactly."

"Where did Simon hear this?"

"I don't know. I told him it was foolishness. That there was no way he could prove it. He, of course, chooses not to listen."

"Where is Simon?"

"His room, probably."

"I called his mobile. He didn't answer."

Miss Abernathy shook her head tiredly. "He turns that off whenever he wants to. I can never reach him if he doesn't want to be reached."

"We'll start at his room, then." Frustration boiled up inside Molly and she worked hard not to let it explode. She didn't like it when a project she was working on didn't go smoothly, and this one was already way beyond.

Stubbornly, the other woman refused to move.

"Miss Abernathy, I'll go without you if I have to. But I think he'll listen to both of us."

With obvious reluctance, Simon's personal assistant found her shoes and jacket and she and Molly went out.

CHAPTER TWENTY

"THERE'S NO DOUBT IN MY MIND that my agency and several others were snookered during the Blackpool Train Robbery." Warren Oatfield-Collins was a serious man in a serious gray suit, and Michael could hear the capital letters in his inflection.

In his fifties, Oatfield-Collins was overweight but still appeared durable and hard. His gray hair lay neatly in place. He smelled of a liberal application of Dunhill aftershave, the same kind that Michael's father wore.

The two men sat at the bar in the Smokehouse and both of them had a pint. Oatfield-Collins had turned down the offer of a booth, stating that he preferred a less formal setting.

"Snookered?"

Oatfield-Collins nodded. "I suppose the current term is *played*. The agencies insuring that shipment were definitely *played*. Snookered. Hoodwinked. Choose your word. The bottom line is that several insurance agencies paid off on bogus claims."

"How many is several?"

"Eight agencies were confirmed to have taken hits."

"For how much money?"

"In the low hundreds of thousands of pounds. For the time, that was quite extensive. With the war on, agencies were facing dire times as it was."

Michael nodded and made notes on his computer. He had

it folded in Tablet PC mode and wrote with a stylus. The computer immediately translated his script into typing.

"Why did you come to Blackpool now?"

"When news of the documentary reached the office, the board of directors wanted an agent to cover it."

"In the event that something turned up."

"Exactly."

"Given the time that's passed, and that most of the people who committed the fraud are now dead, what's the best your agency can hope for?"

"The paintings, Mr. Graham. Bristol and Brinker still owns seventeen of those paintings. If we can find them, they're ours."

"And given current market prices, plus the fact that those paintings have doubtless appreciated in value—"

"Doubtless."

"—your agency stands to make a considerable profit."

"If we can locate the art, yes." Oatfield-Collins's eyes narrowed. "Please don't think that my efforts here are based purely on mercenary interests. It's more than that. The people that run my agency are sons and daughters of the original owners. It doesn't sit well with them that someone bamboozled their fathers and got away with it."

"Do they have any idea who the mastermind behind the robbery was?"

"Three men come to mind at once." The insurance representative ticked them off on his fingers. "Philip Crowe. Richard Sterling. Victor Starkweather. All of them are deceased, but at the time of the robbery they had the resources to pull off an endeavor like this. Crowe and Starkweather were thick as thieves—and neighbors here in Blackpool. They could bribe and buy men to rob the train, and they had the connections to have the forgeries done." He shrugged.

"The favorite at the agency—several of the agencies, actually—was Philip Crowe."

"Because he was closest to the operation."

"It was set up there in his home. Couldn't have been easier. He would have known everything. One way or the other."

"Why Richard Sterling?"

"Because he lost the most paintings."

"His daughter died aboard that train. That would be awfully coldblooded if he masterminded this."

"But not unheard of. And he might have believed she would have been unharmed. We continued to investigate his involvement even after he died and his brother took over the family business."

Michael opened a window and consulted his earlier research. It took him a moment to find the name he was looking for. "Victor Starkweather."

Oatfield-Collins smiled. "The man was practically a pirate during the war. You've read up on him?"

Michael nodded. "Starkweather was caught stealing oil from British tankers and scuttling the ships."

"Exactly, and letting the German navy take the blame for their loss. He was executed at the end of the war. He didn't have any valuables on the train, but that didn't mean that he didn't stage the robbery. The gold bullion would have been enough to spur him on. The paintings, especially if he could hire someone to replicate them, could have been a bonus."

"When did the first forged painting show up?" Michael wanted to draft a timeline if possible.

"Nineteen forty-eight. In Tel Aviv, of all places. Israel had just been made a nation, and money was starting to pour into the area. However, with the Middle East in an uproar, many of the people living there wanted to put their money in something profitable that didn't sit in a bank. Something portable that would hold its value."

"Art."

"Our expert believes that every forgery we've recovered so far was painted by the same man, but not all at the same time. There's a major discrepancy in the materials used."

"How major?"

"Several years, probably."

"That's intriguing." Michael shifted on his seat. "Why wait so long?"

"That's a good question, isn't it?"

"REALLY, MRS. GRAHAM, I'm fairly certain that Mr. Wineguard isn't in his room." Thomas Tidewell managed the Seagull and Sandbar, the bed-and-breakfast Simon was supposed to be staying in. Tidewell was in his early sixties and possessed an elegant charm. He wore a suit and bow tie.

"I just want to be certain that nothing has happened to him. He's been under considerable stress since he's been here." Molly followed the man through the narrow halls of the old rambling house.

"I understand. The terrible death of Mrs. Whiteshire has been disturbing to the whole community. I only met her the evening of her murder, but it's awfully disturbing all the same." Tidewell stopped in front of the door to room six. The brass number shone brilliantly.

Tidewell knocked on the door and called Simon's name. There was no answer.

Molly curbed her impatience. "You met Mrs. Whiteshire that evening?"

The hotelier sorted through the large key ring he held, the clanking echoing in the empty hallway. "Yes, I saw her a little while before I left for the theater."

"Where?"

"Here, of course. I don't get out much. I went to the theater that night for the first time in months." Tidewell found the right key and inserted it into the lock.

"What was Mrs. Whiteshire doing here?" Molly glanced at Miss Abernathy, who quickly glanced away.

"She came calling on Mr. Wineguard." The lock clicked and Tidewell turned the knob.

"Why?"

"I'm quite sure I wouldn't know, Mrs. Graham. I'm not sure how it is in other places, but here at the Seagull and Sandbar we try to provide guests with a modicum of privacy." Tidewell knocked again and got no response. He opened the door a crack. "Mr. Wineguard?"

Still nothing.

Reluctantly, he opened the door. "Mr. Wineguard, I hate to trouble you, but there's been some concern."

Molly followed Tidewell into the room and heard him gasp in astonishment before she saw the wreckage herself. Suitcases had been emptied on the floor and the contents of the closet and wardrobe strewn around the room. The destruction instantly reminded Molly of her ransacked office.

While Tidewell stood frozen, Molly brushed past him and searched the room. Thankfully, after a quick check of the bathroom, Molly confirmed that Simon wasn't there.

"Oh, my God." Miss Abernathy appeared flummoxed. Her anger had vanished, replaced by fear. "We need to find Simon."

Molly couldn't agree more.

She gripped Miss Abernathy's arm and hurried her along through the bed-and-breakfast. "Did you know about Mrs. Whiteshire meeting with Simon?"

"What does it matter? We need to find Simon," the

woman repeated in a panicked voice. Outside, she barely checked the traffic before she strode across the street to the Bear and Viper Pub.

"You can't hold things back from me if I'm going to help," Molly insisted.

"You can't help. If anyone could have made Simon stay away from this, it would have been me. But he wouldn't listen to me. He won't listen to you."

"Why did Mrs. Whiteshire go to see Simon that night?"

Unable to contain the emotions warring within her, Miss Abernathy quivered like a nervous Pomeranian. For a moment Molly feared the woman might explode or pass out on the spot.

"Simon thought she had some information. That she had the key to striking back at Bartholomew Sterling."

"He told you this?"

Miss Abernathy wrapped her arms tightly around herself. "Yes. But he didn't tell me *why* he thought that. From his disappointment after speaking with Mrs. Whiteshire, I gathered that he hadn't learned what he had hoped. That's why I didn't mention it before. I'm trying to remain as loyal as I can under the circumstances."

She wiped away tears that suddenly spilled down her cheeks. "His daughter died in a tragic accident. No one forced her to take those drugs. And if the police could have done something about her death, they would have. Simon just refuses to accept that. He wants someone else to blame, because he can't bear to blame Jenna."

"All right." Molly touched the woman's shoulder. "Let's find Simon. Maybe together we can talk sense into him."

THREE PUBS LATER, MOLLY FELT like giving up. The Blackpool police had arrived at the Seagull and Sandbar, and she had ignored two phone calls from the police department so far. Her feet hurt and she wanted Michael at her side. Whenever things got too turbulent, he was always her rock.

The phone rang again as she and Miss Abernathy walked down an alley behind the latest pub they'd searched. She started to answer the phone, then heard Miss Abernathy yelp in pained shock.

"No!" The woman fled across the alley to a large bin behind a bakery.

Molly started after her, wondering what had caused the reaction. When she spotted a familiar coat partially hanging out of the closed bin, dread clenched a fist around her lungs and made it hard to breathe. By the time she reached Miss Abernathy's side, the woman had dropped her handbag and lifted the heavy lid with both hands.

Inside the bin, Simon Wineguard lay in an inelegant sprawl, arms and legs twisted amid the bags of refuse. His sightless eyes stared up beneath the bullet hole in the center of his forehead.

CHAPTER TWENTY-ONE

MICHAEL SAT IN THE BLACKPOOL Police Station waiting room and tried not to think about Molly being questioned in one of the interview rooms—again.

His mobile vibrated in the pocket of his cargo pants and he fished it out. The caller ID showed Keith's name and number.

"Hello, Keith," he said, unable to keep the weariness out of his voice.

"Hello to you, too, but don't go out of your way to be overjoyed to hear from me."

"Sorry. It's difficult to be joyous about anything when you're sitting in a police station." Michael eyed the woman behind the desk in the corner. She was working at her computer, but she could be listening, doing clerical work or merely passing the hours on Facebook.

"Why are you there?"

"Simon Wineguard, the director of Molly's documentary, has been killed." Michael spoke in a low voice and felt strange doing so. He wasn't used to being suspicious of being observed.

"Who done for him?"

"They don't have any suspects yet. But Molly found the body. The police are questioning her now."

"Is she all right?"

"She is." Michael shifted in the chair and sent a quick

glance at the woman behind the desk. She still seemed focused on the computer.

"I talked to Uncle Morrie. As I suspected, he hasn't got anything on the train robbery."

"That's too bad, but—as you said—not unexpected."

"I showed Uncle Morrie the pictures of those paintings you e-mailed me. *An Afternoon at the Fair?* That we had a little more luck with."

Michael allowed himself to nurse a small hope. He took out his computer and woke it up. The screen came to life and he opened up a sticky note. "What kind of luck?"

"Maybe nothing, but it's worth a try. The time frame you're looking at for the first painting, Uncle Morrie says there's this guy, August Helfers, who was around back then. Guy's gotta be ninety now if he's a day. But during those years he brokered a lot of forgers—guys who had the talent, but they didn't have the connections to sell a painting."

That was new to Michael. "So he was a specialty agent?"

"More or less, mate. Everything has a price. Usually there's somebody who puts a deal together. That's what this guy did. As well as some forgeries of his own."

"Where does he live now?"

"He's here in London. Retired. Got busted by Interpol twenty years ago and they shut him down. Not before he made a fortune, though. He wrote a book on his life as an art forger without naming any names of people that would take offense, and kinda faded away into obscurity. Uncle Morrie says he's a lonely old bloke. Will talk your ear off when he's in his right mind. I got a chat set up with him tomorrow morning."

"Morning? You?"

"Don't sound so disbelieving. You'll hurt my feelings."

"Sorry. That just caught me off guard."

"Right, mate. Anyway, it's a shot in the dark, but it could hit something."

"I think so, too," Michael said, though the idiom was unsettling with recent events. He checked his watch. It was still early afternoon. "Molly and I can be in London tonight. I'm going to talk her into taking a night away from everything. Shouldn't have too much trouble getting her to dodge the media now that Wineguard's been murdered. Maybe I can go over to August Helfers's home with you and chat him up."

"All right."

Michael told Keith he would see him later and rang off. He typed August Helfers's name into Google and quickly turned up information. Wikipedia had an extensive entry on Helfers, citing him as one of the last "gentleman" forgers. In fact, at his trial some of his victims even testified on Helfers's behalf, believing that he'd been hoodwinked as well because he was such a nice person.

"Something interesting catch your eye?"

Recognizing Molly's voice, Michael glanced up. She looked tired and a little shaken. He couldn't imagine what it must have felt like to find someone you knew with a bullet hole in his head.

"Possibly." Michael put the computer on hibernate and shoved it into his bag. "How are you?"

"Tired of being here. I just want to go home."

Standing, Michael took her hand. "Then let's get you home."

"MOLLY?"

Seated in her chair at her desk, Molly opened her eyes and glanced at the doorway. Iris Dunstead stood there with Rachel Donner.

Iris frowned. "Are you sure you're up to company? You could probably use the rest."

"I'm fine." Molly rose and waved the two women to chairs in front of her desk. "Mrs. Donner, it was so good of you to come."

Clasping her big handbag, Rachel Donner sat in one of the chairs. She pulled her sweater a little more tightly around her. "It wasn't a problem. But I'm curious why you asked me to drop by."

"I'll bring tea. That will fortify us all." Iris departed, gently touching Mrs. Donner's shoulder before she left.

"I wanted to talk about Mrs. Whiteshire, if you don't mind." Molly took her seat. "You knew her quite well."

"Her parents and mine were friends after their arrival here. Eventually, Abigail's mum and dad bought a house on the same street as my family's."

"You'd always been friends?"

"Always. I didn't fit into this town very well in the beginning. I lost my family back in London."

Molly remembered the story. Rachel Donner—Beckford then—had been orphaned during the war. The Beckford family had adopted her and raised her as one of their own with their four other children.

"Abigail and I got on at first because we'd talk about what it was like to live in London." Rachel smiled. "Neither of us had any idea, of course. We were far too young to know when we got here on that train."

Iris returned with a tea service and set it on a nearby table. She served out quickly and efficiently without asking how anyone took their tea.

Holding the warm cup in her hands, Molly let the heat soak into her palms for a moment. She was so tired she just wanted to sleep, but her mind wouldn't quit gnawing on the mystery.

"Did Simon Wineguard show any special attention to Mrs. Whiteshire?"

Rachel considered that, her hand trailing absently to the silver rose-shaped pendant she wore, but then shook her head. "Not that I was aware of. But Abigail did pester him a bit. I was afraid she was going to make him angry."

"About what?"

"Abigail was angling for a part in the documentary. Either a role or one of the intros. After all, we were the girls Audrey Cloverfield rescued from the train after her own charge—little heiress Chloe Sterling—perished." Rachel smiled. "When we were girls, Abigail always dreamed about being an actress. She was certain that she would have been in the movies or on stage if she'd remained in London." She paused. "I always told her she could do it. But I guess neither one of us ended up having the life we'd intended to. She married badly again and again. She never was quite happy with her lot. But she was my friend."

"You were a good friend to her." Iris patted the other woman on the arm. "She thought a lot of you, you know."

"I do know." Rachel brushed tears from her eyes. "For a while, we roomed together. After we left home and before our first marriages. It was convenient. Both of us wore the same size clothing. Abigail used to say that our wardrobes were doubled just because of our friendship. We could each buy dresses and take turns wearing them." She sipped her tea. "Those were good days."

"Did she tell you she was going to Simon Wineguard's room at the Seagull and Sandbar that Friday afternoon?"

"Yes. Abigail was hoping to talk to Mr. Wineguard about a spot in the documentary again. She hadn't given up. I don't think she ever would have."

"He agreed to see her, or she just went over?"

"Oh, he agreed to see her. In fact, he *wanted* to see her. He asked her to bring a particular photograph with her."

Molly's breath caught. They had taken dozens of photographs, and video, of the people and sites that would be involved in the documentary—and that material had been the only things missing from her office and Iris's home.

"What photograph?"

Rachel shrugged. "It was one of the group of survivors."

Molly had taken multiple shots because getting all the survivors together in one spot had been problematic.

She brought up the computer files with the images she'd printed out. Luckily she had made digital backups of everything. After turning the monitor so Rachel could see it, Molly slowly brought up the images.

"I don't know." Frustration tightened the woman's mouth and eyes. "They all look the same."

Molly silently agreed. "You're sure Simon was specific?"

"He was. Abigail went through her pictures carefully." Rachel leaned forward and nodded. "This one. I believe it was this one."

The image on the monitor showed all seven survivors standing in front of the Blackpool Library. Molly couldn't see anything remarkable about the picture. Abigail Whiteshire and Rachel Donner stood next to each other, both smiling brightly.

"See how radiant she was?" Rachel spoke in a rasp, her voice thick with emotion. "Abigail was so excited that she was finally going to be a star. That's not how it turned out, though, is it?"

CHAPTER TWENTY-TWO

AFTER RACHEL HAD LEFT WITH Irwin, who was driving her home, Molly studied the picture and tried to divine Simon's interest. All she got was frustrated.

"If you keep staring at the monitor like that, your face will freeze with that expression." Iris gathered up the tea service.

Molly shot the woman a grimace.

"That one would be even worse, if you want my opinion."

"Not particularly. But I would appreciate your insight about this picture. Why would Simon be so captivated by it?"

Iris came to stand behind Molly and gazed at the image for a time in silence. "It's seven elderly people. That's all."

"Seven very extraordinary people when you consider that train wreck." Molly tapped a fingernail on her keyboard. "But Simon had already seen this. Why would he want to look at it again?"

"Maybe he didn't have a copy of it."

"Miss Abernathy and I kept all the files, so why would he need one? And if he did, why would he ask Mrs. Whiteshire to bring it to him instead of me? Or Miss Abernathy for that matter?"

Frowning a little, Iris inclined her head. "That is a question, isn't it?"

"Did anything Simon ever talked to you about strike you as odd?"

"Not really. He questioned me about what I remembered from the train wreck, but of course it wasn't much. I was far too young. And I didn't have a story like Abigail and Rachel."

"What do you mean?"

"I wasn't pulled from the wreckage by the teenage hero, Audrey Cloverfield."

A connection skittered through Molly's thoughts and she tried to grab it. "Rachel mentioned her, too. Who was Audrey Cloverfield again?"

"She was the nanny for Chloe Sterling." Iris sighed. "Poor child. And I mean both of them, actually. I think Audrey was only sixteen at the time."

"What happened to her?"

"She was injured, but she survived. But I can't imagine how devastating it was to lose that little girl."

"Where is she now?"

"I've no idea. She'd be almost ninety, if she's still alive."

"SHE'S STILL ALIVE."

Pausing in his packing, Michael glanced up at Molly. His wife was smiling and excited, which was a grand change from earlier in the day. However, something this dramatic warranted an explanation.

"Are you all right, love?"

"No, not even. Truthfully, I'm more incensed than ever." Molly looked at the open gym bag on their bed. "What are you doing?"

"Packing. We're taking a road trip to London. I'm meeting with Keith. You're dodging the media and going shopping to relax. Does any of that sound familiar?"

"Yes. Sorry. Let me help." Molly crossed the floor and took over the packing. She immediately removed everything Michael had put in the bag and began reorganizing it.

Michael lay on the bed and watched as she arranged his bag to her specifications. Thankfully she left all his choices. Though she did add some of her own from his closet.

"You should look your best meeting Mr. Helfers tomorrow."

"The man's a retired thief."

"But you're not. Dress nice."

Michael rolled his eyes, turned over onto his back, and feigned being mortally wounded.

Molly held up a blue silk shirt with an abbreviated collar. "If it's overcast in London tomorrow, wear this."

Michael realized he'd diverted Molly from her earlier excitement. "Who's alive?"

Molly folded the shirt and carefully put it into the gym bag. "Audrey Cloverfield. And she lives in London."

"Chloe Sterling's nanny?" That surprised Michael.

"I know I shouldn't be amazed that you can just pluck her name from the air like that, but I am."

"I have mad researcher skills, love."

"That mutant ability is still bothersome to the rest of us normal people."

"What's so interesting about her?"

"I believe she is the only adult survivor remaining from the train robbery."

Michael rifled his mental files and came to the same conclusion. "Probably."

"But it's strange that Simon didn't ask her to be part of the documentary…."

"Did he even know she was alive? You obviously didn't until a few minutes ago. I hadn't considered it, either."

"I hadn't thought about it. She might not be healthy enough to travel." Finished with the bag, Molly zipped it closed and sat on the bed. "I'm sure Simon would have discovered her in his research and you'd think he would want some kind of input from her."

"Maybe she didn't want to relive the tragedy of losing that little girl again." Michael reached for Molly and pulled her back into his arms. "That's not the kind of thing you ever get over. Not even after all this time."

"Probably not. Still, I'd like to ask her. She lives in London, and we're going there anyway." Molly kissed him and pushed him away. "Let's go."

CHAPTER TWENTY-THREE

"YOU SO SHOULD HAVE KEPT ME from getting knackered last night, mate. You're supposed to look out for me." Keith stopped at the door of his apartment complex and pulled on a pair of dark sunglasses. He tugged back his jacket sleeve to reveal a bare arm. "And, God, look at this—it's still morning."

Keith Larkin was a weight lifter and spent several evenings a week in the gym. He was cut and chiseled, brown haired and brown eyed. He wore a short-cropped full beard.

"Not hardly." Michael stepped out onto the stoop into the city's familiar overcast. "It's quarter past ten. I've been up for three hours."

Despite the lack of sleep, he'd spent the time going over his notes regarding August Helfers and the paintings Oakfield-Collins had told him about. The insurance agent had forwarded other relevant newspaper stories about artwork from the Blackpool Train Robbery that had proven to be forgeries, as well. Apparently they were working on shared knowledge at the moment, but Michael was certain that would change the instant Oatfield-Collins decided sharing didn't benefit his agency.

"I haven't willingly seen a quarter past ten unless I stayed up that long since you moved from London. Seriously, mate, I don't know how you do it." Keith yawned.

"I like to work, and when I'm not working, I like to play.

One of those two things will get me up and going every morning."

"And you have Molly." Keith grinned. "As I recall, she's changed some of your layabout ways. Morning person and all."

Michael smiled. "Maybe a little."

The flat where August Helfers lived was in Mayfair. They took the tube out and Michael had to endure the press of bodies standing in the car. The mixture of body odor, soap, perfume and bad breath cascaded over him. The crowded environment was another thing he'd been glad to get away from.

After a brisk twelve-minute walk, they stepped inside the building foyer, buzzed Helfers's flat and were let in. Helfers met them at the door. He was dressed in tan slacks and a dark red smoking jacket that had gone out of style years ago, but he wore it with accustomed ease.

"Mr. Graham?" Robust and in his early eighties, Helfers had a firm grip and an easy manner. He was bald except for a fringe of gray hair, and he had a perfectly groomed mustache.

"I'm Michael Graham. Please call me Michael." Releasing the man's hand, Michael stepped into the flat while Helfers greeted Keith.

Wood paneling in the living room made the room dark, and heavy drapes kept the sun at bay to prevent damage to the numerous paintings that filled the wall.

"You've got quite the collection, don't you?" Michael stepped over to one of the paintings he recognized. It showed a boy with a pipe sitting in front of a wall of roses. A garland of blossoms circled the boy's head. "Picasso. From his Rose Period."

Helfers joined Michael in front of the painting. "Very good. *Garçon à la Pipe. Boy with a Pipe.*"

"Not an original, I assume."

Helfers chuckled. "No. A very good copy, but not the original. That one sold at Sotheby's not long ago for one hundred four million. It set a new record."

Keith cursed good naturedly. "I'm in the wrong business."

"You're an artist?"

"I am." Keith pointed at the painting. "And I could have painted you one of these where the boy's arms were symmetrical. His left is a lot longer than his right."

"Ah, but then you wouldn't be Picasso, now would you?" Helfers studied the painting. "It was his use of color and shape that really made his career."

"Maybe so."

"And he was a workaholic. He created over fifty thousand works during his career. More of Picasso's paintings have been stolen than any other artist."

Michael shook his head. "Really?"

"I've got a Van Gogh Sunflowers on the other wall." Helfers smoothed his mustache and looked across the room. "Not the original, either, of course, but a nice copy. Personally, I believe it is one of the copies Van Gogh made of his own work, but I haven't been able to prove it. That inability has been one of my greatest disappointments." He smiled. "Maybe one day." He returned his gaze to Michael. "But you didn't come here to hear me talk about this art. You have some paintings you're interested in."

"You're familiar with the Blackpool Train Robbery?"

Helfers waved at them to accompany him to the couches in the center of the room. A tea service sat waiting on the table. "Of course. One of the better stings in the art world." He sat and poured tea into cups.

"You say it like it's common knowledge." Michael accepted his cup and said thank you. He took out a micro-recorder and asked if he could use it.

Helfers nodded permission. "At the time, it wasn't widely accepted or known. Let me assure you of that. It wasn't till later, when the forgeries started popping up in the hands of collectors and the law enforcement people, that the truth came out. Or, at least, guessed at. And everyone involved just as quickly started burying it because no one wanted to deal with such an issue during the war. Afterward…well, afterward no one wanted to deal with it in the public eye, either. A bunch of rich people crying over their losses when the country was in tatters wouldn't have gone over well. Especially since insurance paid off so handsomely. Philip Crowe did a very good job of covering up his operation."

"You know for a fact that Philip Crowe was behind the robbery?" Michael asked.

"I can't prove it. Neither can any of the insurance agents that worked the robbery. But everyone assumed Philip Crowe was guilty of masterminding the whole thing. After all, he had access."

"Because he was working with the military to secure the train."

"Exactly." Helfers leaned back in his seat and sipped tea.

"But he didn't have art on the train."

"The speculation was that Philip Crowe had organized the whole robbery to get a few people a payoff from the insurance agencies. And then he stole the art from his friends. Since their losses were eventually recovered through insurance policies, he could claim there was no foul."

"And he got the original paintings."

"If it happened like that, yes."

"Then why did the forgeries start surfacing?"

Helfers played with an onyx ring on his right hand,

sliding it on and off. "The art business is very incestuous and narcissistic." He waved at the room. "You only have to look at this collection to realize that. After the robbery, there would have been people wanting to buy the stolen art. There always are. Avid collectors will hover like vultures, hoping to get a bargain before the original owners or the insurance agencies can arrange a buy-back. Obviously someone sought to capitalize on the potential created by the robbery. Because the event was highly publicized, other art collectors knew what had been taken. And they knew that at least some of what was taken couldn't be insured. Trust me when I say that not all of those people were scrupulous. A great opportunity to market forgeries."

"But eventually the buyers discovered they were getting ripped off."

"Yes."

"Would you have handled something like this?" Michael felt uneasy and embarrassed to ask the question, but he needed a point of reference.

"No. I was convicted for being in receivership of stolen art. Art, not forgeries." Helfers smiled at the memory. "I have never and would never pass off a forgery as an original. However, I have brokered deals for several successful forgeries clients wanted. In fact, several museums have forgeries in their collections and are fully aware they have them. There are just too many circulating these days."

Keith leaned forward. "My uncle Morrie told me you might have an idea of the artist that did these." He opened the folder Michael had brought and spread out the pictures.

Helfers took a pair of glasses from the inside of his jacket pocket and slid them into place. He pointed to *An Afternoon at the Fair*. "Ah, yes. I thought I recognized this one when you mentioned the piece. Especially when you told me it had been found twice."

Helfers took his time examining the other photos and made appreciative noises.

"These are very good. It's hard to be sure how many painters were involved. Could be as few as one, but no more than three or four."

"Do you know who copied *An Afternoon at the Fair?*" Michael curbed his enthusiasm, but it was difficult.

"I believe I do." Helfers picked up the photo and studied it a little more. "There was a man named Byron Kirkwell. Not a particularly inspired painter. He lacked the eye for original work, but he was an excellent reproductionist."

"Forger, you mean." Keith grinned. "I mean no offense. Just trying to keep it simple, mate."

"Skills are always for sale, young man. And talent is what it is. Comic book artists are highly regarded in some circles, and I've seen their original art sell for high prices." Helfers put the picture back on the table. "I take no offense, nor do I apologize for my career choice. Kirkwell was a child prodigy by all accounts, but he was also egotistical. He couldn't help signing his work."

"The signature is there…" Michael leaned in more closely and inspected the picture of the painting. "It was of the original artist. Not Kirkwell."

"Here. In the tower." Helfers used his manicured forefinger to indicate a small section of the girders in the Eiffel Tower. There, barely detectable even after Helfers pointed it out, were two letters formed by the hollows between girders: *BK.*

"I hadn't noticed that." Michael took out his camera and snapped a close-up shot of the "signature." "I'm impressed."

"Kirkwell's initials, of course." Helfers leaned back and picked up his tea.

"You spotted that rather quickly, mate." Keith kept the brunt of accusation out of his voice, but Michael was certain his friend was as suspicious as he was.

Helfers shrugged and didn't seem guilty or offended. "I've developed a trained eye. Once I recognized the handiwork, I knew what I was looking for. You came here today to take advantage of my expertise."

"What can you tell us about Byron Kirkwell?" Michael asked.

"Not a lot, I'm afraid. His personal life was very closed off. Most of the people in this trade try to avoid the limelight, you see."

"Of course."

"Is there anyone else I could ask about him?"

"Up until last week, you could have talked to him yourself."

"What do you mean?"

"Kirkwell was still alive until last week. Then, last Friday, he was struck and killed by a car when he stepped off the curb."

Michael turned cold. Abigail Whiteshire had been murdered last Friday. Byron Kirkwell had also been killed. And now Simon.

Michael wasn't a big believer in coincidences. Video game players didn't like them and he personally felt that coincidences were a crutch.

So if everything was connected, what had the catalyst been?

CHAPTER TWENTY-FOUR

"DOESN'T APPEAR TO BE MUCH here." Keith shook his head morosely as he stared at his notebook computer. "Old guy doesn't pay attention to where he's going, steps off a curb and gets hit by a car. End of story. Surprised it even made the news."

Michael stretched for a moment, then took a deep breath to relax. Not much of Byron Kirkwell's death had hit the media. There was no television coverage, and the newspaper pieces he'd researched on the Internet gave nothing more than Kirkwell's name, age and place of residence.

"Kind of creepy that it happened not far from where I live, though. Really didn't need that grim reminder right around the corner, so to speak." Keith eyed his empty glass. "Why don't I get us another pint?"

"All right." Frustrated, Michael gazed around the small pub not far from Helfers's flat and willed his mind to work.

The morning crowd loitered and watched a sports game on the wide-screen television over the bar. An older female bartender kept a running dialogue going with some of the obvious regulars.

Michael pulled up the obituary because it had more salient information than anything else he'd read. Byron Kirkwell had been survived by one granddaughter and three great-grandchildren. The granddaughter lived in the East End, as well.

"Your brow's all furrowed, mate." Keith set the pints down on the tabletop, then pointed to his head. "I know that look. You're thinking something, but you don't like what you're thinking."

After taking a sip of his beer, Michael nodded. "Helfers believes Kirkwell painted some—if not all—the forgeries that turned up."

Keith sat and laced his hands behind his head. He was used to playing devil's advocate to Michael. "Even if you don't want to take the bloke's word for it, there are those initials."

"I know." Michael inhaled and let his mind spin. "If Wineguard did touch a nerve in his investigation for the documentary, and I'm still not sure if that's true, then Kirkwell would have been at risk."

"A crime seventy years gone?" Keith shook his head. "Would it really matter at this point?"

"The gold belonged to the British military. They're long on memory and short on forgiveness."

"Okay. But how many of those folks involved with that train robbery are still alive?"

Michael shook his head. "But maybe the government would make a greater effort at reclamation if they discovered who was behind the robbery."

"If Philip Crowe was the mastermind, it would give this Aleister Crowe bloke something to fret about. Could be why he was so intent on Molly and her documentary. And it wasn't just the British government, mate. Bartholomew Sterling and some of them other art owners had a bone or two to pick with him, as well."

"If Philip Crowe hired Kirkwell to forge the paintings, that could make Kirkwell a liability."

"Might mean stepping off that curb last week wasn't an

accident." Keith frowned. "Doesn't take much to shove an old man out in front of a car."

"That thought crossed my mind."

"It's all those video games you play, mate. Makes you see plot and intrigue everywhere."

Michael grinned at the jibe. "Kirkwell has a surviving family member."

"A granddaughter." Keith nodded.

"Maybe I should call her. See if I could talk to her."

"All she can say is no. Funeral was two days ago."

"I could be disturbing her for no reason."

"You could be. Probably are. But are you going to be able to go back to Blackpool without turning over that particular rock?" Keith grinned. "I know you, mate. You can't ever leave well enough alone."

"Especially not if Molly's caught in the cross fire." Michael searched the woman's name on Google and found a phone number for her. He took out his iPhone and called.

PENNY TORRINGTON LIVED in a flat with her husband and three children. By the time Michael and Keith got to her home, the kids were out of school but her husband was still on his bus route.

"Please sit." Penny pointed to the couch in the small living room. She was in her late twenties, brunette and slim. She wore lavender hospital scrubs. "I don't have much time, I'm afraid. I'm going on shift practically the minute my husband arrives home."

"That's all right, Mrs. Torrington. This won't take long." Michael leaned forward and put his elbows on his knees.

"You said this was about my grandfather?"

"Yes."

Penny shrugged. "I can't tell you much about him. He came around every now and again to visit me and the kids.

My husband didn't care for him and was sometimes rude about it. But Mr. Kirkwell said we were all the family he had left and that meant something." She paused and tears glimmered in her blue eyes. "I hate that he didn't mean more to us, but he didn't. It's really sad. It's just one of those things that happens in a family, I suppose."

"You knew he was an artist?" Michael felt uncomfortable asking questions. It was strange how easily it all came to him, and he suspected it was from watching too many police shows on television.

"Yes. He gave the children paintings of clowns and fantasy creatures. The kids weren't sure what to do with him, either, but he was nice to them."

"Did the police talk to you about his death?"

"No." Suspicion stiffened the woman's features and she drew back. "Should they have?"

"Not at all."

"Seems an odd question to ask, Mr. Graham. You never did say what you were after about Mr. Kirkwell."

"I'll try to explain." Michael hesitated a moment, then decided to just tell the truth. "We believe your grandfather was involved in a train robbery near Blackpool."

Penny frowned and looked uncomfortable. "The one that's been mentioned on the telly lately?"

"Yes. Did he ever mention it?"

"Mr. Graham, I don't mean to sound abrupt, but that's not something that Mr. Kirkwell and I would ever talk about. I was aware that he was a criminal and had been arrested a number of times, and even been to prison. That's one of the reasons I wanted to keep my distance from him, and why Bob doesn't—didn't—trust him. We didn't feel he would be a good influence on the children." Penny shook her head. "If Mr. Kirkwell hadn't been so melancholy and so alone, I probably would have turned him away. But I couldn't. Not after my mother died four years ago. She was the only one really close to him, and that wasn't good, either. He was like an old tomcat on his last legs. You could just tell."

"Had he been acting any differently lately?"

Penny thought for a moment. "Actually, he came to see me a few days before he—the accident. He was acting nervous, fidgety. But he sometimes was that way. He was an alcoholic, and had tried to quit. Didn't want to come around the children breathing fumes."

"One of my granddads was the same way." Keith shrugged. "Just couldn't stay away from the stuff."

"Then you understand."

Keith nodded.

"Anyway, Mr. Kirkwell told me that he knew he wasn't going to leave much in this world. He seemed so maudlin that I wanted to help him. Try to find some worth in him. I suggested that he would leave something behind—all the paintings he'd done. He cried a little then, and it was so sad. He said that his best work couldn't be claimed, and that it wasn't even his. I didn't understand what he was talking about."

"The forgeries he'd done."

"Possibly. I just know that it was heartbreaking for him. He said he was never that good of a painter. In the end, his vision was failing and his hand wasn't steady anymore— made it harder to paint, you see. But he gave me a stack of journals. Made me promise to keep them, that he wanted someone to remember him after he was gone. I tried to refuse but he insisted. Bob was furious with me for accepting them, but he had already moved them from his home to ours. I told Bob I'd take them back to Mr. Kirkwell at some point, but that was the last time I saw him. Till I identified him for the police, that is."

Michael clamped down on the surge of hope he felt. Artists and writers habitually made sketches and notes about projects, always planning on paper before they approached the final effort.

"Do you still have those journals?"

Penny nodded. "Yes."

"Could I possibly see them?"

Penny led them to her hall closet, where she pulled a large box out from behind a line of coats. The box was open, and as Michael bent to examine the journals he saw that they had been beaten by time and hard use. All forty-one of them were ink-spattered and most had rolled spines. Strings tied them shut.

"It's depressing that all a man had to show for himself after a long life can be stuffed into a box like that," she commented.

Michael knelt and rifled through the box in the hallway. "A lot of people leave nothing of themselves behind."

"You're right. I suppose it could be worse." Penny glanced at her watch. "Bob will be home soon. I should be getting the meal ready for him and the children."

"I'd like to read these journals if I could. Perhaps borrow them for a while. I'd be glad to pay you a rental fee."

"Just tell me you can find a place for them, Mr. Graham. Bob really doesn't want them in the house, and I haven't a clue what to do with them. But I can't bear the thought of simply throwing them away." She gazed at the box of journals. "No matter what else they may be, those books are the sum of Mr. Kirkwell's life."

"We have a library in Blackpool." Michael stood up. "If it turns out that Mr. Kirkwell did have something to do with that train robbery, maybe they can make a home for them there. If not, I'll find another place for them."

"Just give me your word, then."

"You have it, Penny."

A smile briefly lighted the woman's face, then quickly went away. "I hope you don't mind if I wish that you're wrong about Mr. Kirkwell's involvement, and that they won't stay in Blackpool."

Michael nodded and smiled. "I don't mind."

"You realize you owe me bloody big for all of this, don't you?" Keith set one of the two boxes they'd divided Kirkwell's journals into on a table in a pub round the corner from the Torrington residence. "Dragging me out of bed and me hungover, then turning me into a beast of burden."

"A beast of burden would have carried everything and not been a pain in the arse about it." Michael took off his jacket and hung it on the back of a chair, then he sat. "And I wouldn't be buying a beast of burden a few pints for his trouble, now would I?"

Keith grinned. "No, mate, you wouldn't." He flagged down a passing server.

After only a few minutes searching, it became apparent that the journals weren't in any particular order, nor were they all dated or identified. Evidently Kirkwell had struggled with sobriety, but still he'd managed to keep the journals.

Michael and Keith sorted out the early ones first.

"He had a gift, mate. Had a good eye in the beginning." Keith leafed through one of the journals. "Not quite so talented with composition. But he could copy someone else's work like nobody's business." He showed Michael a rendering of the Mona Lisa.

"He had a hand for faces, too." Michael held open a journal with street scenes of London.

A shoeshine boy with brushes and rags worked on a

gentleman's shoes. A policeman in the midst of a car wreck blew furiously on his whistle. An old lady carrying a shopping bag walked along an alley. In each of the scenes, the subjects' eyes held a deep, haunting emotion.

"You know what he needed, don't you, mate?" Keith's voice was sober. "A chance. That's all. If someone had seen him before he racked up a criminal record, he could have gone another way."

"Yeah."

Halfway into their second pint, Keith held up another book. "Hey. Isn't this that creepy lighthouse in Blackpool?"

Michael dragged his attention from the journal he was going through and gazed at the page. A lighthouse stood on a rocky promontory in the sketch.

At first Michael thought the drawing couldn't be of the Glower Lighthouse because there wasn't a pub at the bottom. Then he remembered the pub hadn't been built onto the lighthouse until the 1960s.

"Yeah, maybe."

Keith turned a few more pages and stopped. Wordlessly, he showed the page to Michael. It was the same scene Michael had viewed dozens of times recently—the Blackpool train wreck.

But there was something about Byron Kirkwell's inked sketch that brought out the horror of that day more powerfully than any other image Michael had seen.

CHAPTER TWENTY-FIVE

MOLLY SAID GOODBYE TO Michael and took the tube to the Elephant and Castle station, then walked the rest of the way to Audrey Cloverfield's building. The Blackpool police had given up following them at the town limits and she and Michael had left the car in a parking area in a protected lot in London proper.

After an unsuccessful Internet search, Molly concluded that Audrey Cloverfield either didn't have a phone or had an unlisted number. She felt bad that she couldn't call and let the woman know she was coming, but was no less determined to meet her.

Audrey Cloverfield lived in a second-floor walk-up. The neighborhood had once been a decent sort, but those days were over. Pockets of London continued to rot away as maintenance became too expensive and the economy struggled. Around the corner on a signpost, one of the bright red statues of an elephant with a castle turret on its back that marked the neighborhood made everything look cheerier.

Building security was nonexistent. Molly entered the foyer and climbed the stairs on her right. On her way up, she tried to figure out what she was going to say to the woman. *Hello, Mrs. Cloverfield. We haven't met, but I'm here to talk to you about the Blackpool train wreck. You know, the one where your young charge, Chloe Sterling, died?*

The greeting needed work. Molly hoped that she could

simply wing it when the time came. She paused in front of the door and lifted her hand to knock. Then she spotted the thin cracks of splintered wood on the doorjamb and paint flecks on the floor.

Panic spread through Molly and she willed herself to walk away. She'd seen too many movies where characters met bad ends by going through doorways that obviously shouldn't have been gone through.

Just turn around and go back down the stairs.

Molly did turn, and started reaching into her handbag for her mobile with the intention of calling the police.

Then a big man in slacks, a pullover and a jacket stood in front of her and blocked her way. He was solidly built, probably in his late thirties or early forties. His face was broad, apelike, and a scar tracked his right cheek. Lank black hair hung down over his low forehead.

He grinned, exposing a gold bridge beneath the snarled scar that pulled at his lip. "Hello, pretty bird." He nodded toward the door. "What say me an' you go inside? That's what you come 'ere for, right? For the old bag what lived inside?"

"I've got the wrong door." Molly tried to keep the panic out of her voice, but she knew she hadn't managed it when her brittle words cracked.

"No, you ain't." The man's face went cold and hard. "I was warned you might come sniffin' round 'ere. So I waited for you a bit. And 'ere you are. Now let's go on inside."

Molly screamed and the big man grabbed for her. Reacting instinctively, she brought up the small canister of pepper spray attached to her key ring and tried to douse her attacker. In her haste, she dropped her handbag and mostly missed him. The spray hit his shoulder, but the noxious cloud filled the air between them with burning fumes.

Eyes watering and lungs racked with sudden spasms, Molly tried to bolt. The man roared in rage and flung his arms wide to stop her. Partly blinded and disoriented by the pepper spray, he slid his hand over her shoulder, but he managed to trap her against the door all the same.

Molly struggled to scream again but the choking haze of the pepper spray had robbed her voice. She felt the door behind her, groped for the knob, found it, twisted and almost fell as she stumbled inside the flat.

The man cursed at her and followed. But he misjudged the doorway and banged off the frame, then rebalanced and charged inside.

Molly turned and ran, barely registering the horror all around her. An elderly woman's body lay tumbled on the floor. She wore a long housecoat and a petrified expression. Her white hair fanned out in disarray across the rug. Purple bruises ringed her throat.

Fueled by adrenaline, Molly ran for the first door on the right. If her pursuer hadn't tripped over something on the floor, she might not have made it. Willing her fingers to work quickly, she locked the door behind her.

She was in a small bedroom. The bed was made and pictures hung on the wall. A bookshelf overflowed with paperback novels. Knitting sat in a basket, watched over by three blue ceramic cats.

The man thumped into the door behind Molly, but it held. He yelled curses and vile threats and slammed against it again.

Molly knew the lock or the door would eventually yield to his strength. And if the neighbors had heard the violence, they might not want to get involved. Cursing the fact that she'd dropped her handbag—with her phone in it—she prayed someone would call the police.

It won't be in time. Save yourself.

Spotting the window, Molly pushed herself from the door and crossed the room in three strides. She tried the latch on the window and was immediately relieved when it loosened. The door came off the hinges at the exact moment she got the window up. The man lunged after her as she hurled herself through the window onto the metal landing. She got to her feet, barely evading his desperate attempt to catch her.

Terrified, Molly kicked off her heels and sprinted down the fire escape to the alley. Her breath came in rapid gasps but she still couldn't yell for help. The metal stairs vibrated under her as the big man tumbled out onto the landing, as well. Even barefooted, Molly raced like a deer across the rough alley. Sharp pain bit into her feet but she didn't give in to it.

Six more long strides put her past the entrance of the alley and out to the street. She wheeled to her left and ran into pedestrian traffic. A man tried to grab her and she fought him off, realizing too late that he was only trying to keep her from falling.

"It's okay." He held his hands up and backed away. A handful of people stopped to look. "Just didn't see you there is all."

She spun around, breath rushing through her throat, searching for her attacker. He hurtled around the corner, saw the crowd and quickly retreated.

Molly turned to the man who had tried to help her. "Can you call the police?" she croaked, relieved to hear the sound of her voice. "Please? Tell them there's been a murder in flat 207."

BY THE TIME MOLLY RETURNED to Audrey Cloverfield's door, a crowd had gathered. Most of them were neighbors and appeared upset. Calmly, Molly retrieved her handbag from the floor—grateful it hadn't spilled or been noticed—and pushed through, hoping her attacker wasn't back inside the room.

A man in the group caught her arm. "Who are you?" He stared at her suspiciously.

"Molly Graham. I came here to see Mrs. Cloverfield." Gently, Molly removed her arm from his grasp. "I discovered her."

Another voice from the crowd whispered, "She's the woman I saw in the alley."

"Did she kill Audrey?" said another.

"There was someone else in there. A man."

Molly turned to the group. "Did anyone recognize the man that was in the alley?"

No one answered.

Steeling herself, she entered Audrey Cloverfield's flat again.

"You really shouldn't be in there, miss." A thin man in a black T-shirt and jeans lounged against the doorway. His hair was long and he had a wild goatee. Tattoos covered his forearms. "The coppers don't like you interferin' in a crime scene."

"I'm not interfering."

"Walkin' in there, bold as brass—some would call that interferin'."

"Did you know Mrs. Cloverfield?"

"I did things for 'er now an' then. I do things for a lot of the women in this buildin'. Packages. Groceries. The post. Like that."

"So you were in her flat a lot?"

The man held his hands up. "If you're tryin' to tie me into this—"

"No, I just was wondering if you could tell if anything is missing? Was this a robbery?"

Cautiously, the man entered the room and gazed around. "Nothin' missin'. Mrs. Cloverfield, she was a lady stayed by herself a lot. Didn't entertain much. Wasn't much in 'ere to nick."

Another woman, one in her sixties or seventies, entered the room. Tears filled her eyes as she stared down at the dead woman. She put a hand to her mouth.

"Poor, poor dear."

Molly's heart continued to hammer in her chest. She wanted Michael there with her. He was only a call away, but there wasn't time. She forced her fear away and studied the room. The murder hadn't been random. Otherwise, the killer wouldn't have been there waiting for her.

He'd said someone had warned him about her. But who? It was something to puzzle over, and she immediately realized she was more vulnerable than she'd thought.

A small Bible lay on the floor, probably knocked off the nearby side table. A photograph peeked from beneath the cover, and the thing that caught Molly's attention was the structure in the background. The photograph was in black and white, but she still recognized Glower Lighthouse.

However, she didn't recognize the little girl in the photograph.

"The coppers are here."

"Police." The voice was stern, used to being obeyed.

People at the doorway shifted. The man in the black T-shirt seemed to melt away.

Reaching down quickly, Molly picked up the Bible and put it back on the small table. Deftly, she pocketed the photograph and stood just before the first uniformed policeman stepped through the door.

"You." The constable pointed at Molly. "Come out of there."

DCI ABNER SMOLLET WAS AN overworked man, but careful about his investigations. He sat on the other side of the interview table and studied Molly under heavy-lidded eyes. The fluorescent lights gleamed off his bald head. His thin neck was wattled as a turkey's.

"You've never met the victim before, Mrs. Graham?"

"No." Molly was calmer than she'd expected, but then it had been a most unusual week. Still, she was grateful Michael waited somewhere outside.

"And you came to London because you thought she might be able to shed some light on these murders in Blackpool?" Smollet glanced at his notes.

"Yes."

The policeman sipped the cup of tea he'd brought with him. "I've spoken with DCI Paddington and he vouches for you."

Molly waited, unsure of what to say to that.

"I'm going to take your statement as it stands. I don't see any reason to detain you further."

"Thank you."

Smollet laced his fingers. "What did you hope to learn from Miss Cloverfield?"

"She's—she *was*—the only person I'm aware of who was old enough to remember the Blackpool Train Robbery. I just wanted to talk to her."

Smollet referred to his notes again. "Wouldn't this other gentleman, Mr. Simon Wineguard, be the one to interview her about the documentary?"

"I'd heard he did, but I wasn't privy to that conversation."

"He didn't relay the information?"

"No."

Carefully, Smollet added a few printed lines to his notepad. "I'm going to stay in touch with DCI Paddington regarding his investigation and mine. We may need to bring you in again."

"Of course." Nervousness filled Molly as she thought about the photograph she had in her pocket. According to everything she had discovered about Audrey Cloverfield, the woman had left no family behind. That fact made the photograph of the little girl even more curious.

CHAPTER TWENTY-SIX

"YOU REALIZE YOU COULD get arrested for what you've done?" Michael stared at his wife in disbelief.

"Taking a photograph that will most likely end up donated to a thrift shop or thrown away entirely?" Molly shook her head. "A slap on the wrist at most—if the police ever found out. And I don't intend them to."

"What if this Detective Smollet character had found the photograph on you?"

"I would have said I was going to ask Miss Cloverfield about it. Smollet wouldn't have known I didn't have it when I went there."

A grimace tightened Michael's mouth and he didn't try to keep it from showing. "Deceit is coming far too easily to you, love."

"If the stakes weren't so high, I would never even consider doing some of the things I've done these past few days."

Michael tried to think of a rejoinder, couldn't, and finally gave up. There was no arguing with her logic.

Sitting across the table from them, Keith chuckled. "I missed this. Watching the two of you squabble."

Michael shot his friend a warning glare.

"Oh, sod off, mate. You've spent the morning dragging me around to the homes of known criminals while playing detective. Molly went to see an old lady. If anyone should have gotten into trouble, it was us. And we're lucky it wasn't."

Neon lights that fronted the pub's windows threw hazy colors over them in the corner booth. As usual, Keith had gotten out an artist's pad and started sketching. Images paraded across the paper, many of them the faces of Penny Torrington and August Helfers. A few were of Molly and Michael, as well.

Keith had a point, but Molly's close call bothered him. A server came over to ask if they wanted another round of drinks. Michael opted for tea and Molly coffee, but Keith had another pint.

"This has gotten out of hand, love." Michael worked to keep his voice level. "We're in way over our heads and I think it's time we admitted that."

"We were in over our heads from the start, but that doesn't mean I'm going to sit on the sidelines."

Michael sighed and searched for an argument that didn't sound like an argument. He wasn't very successful.

"Three people have died because of this documentary." Emotion vibrated in Molly's voice, and Michael detected both pain and guilt. "A documentary that I initiated."

"This isn't your fault, love. This situation isn't yours to take on."

"Then whose is it?" Her eyes locked on his and he realized she wasn't going to back away from the course she'd set for herself.

"Paddington and this man Smollet—"

"We can give them what we've uncovered so far. If they can do something with that information, I'm glad."

"All right." Michael let out a long breath. "Let's go over all that we do know."

"We've established that this man Kirkwell was involved

in the Blackpool Train Robbery. Those sketches you found in his journal prove that."

Michael took the journal from his bag and opened it on the table. When she'd called him about being questioned by the police regarding Miss Cloverfield's death, he'd filled her in briefly about Kirkwell and the journals.

He continued, "Kirkwell possibly worked for Philip Crowe, and Crowe shows up a lot in the sketches Kirkwell made at the time of the robbery." Michael opened the journal to one of the pages he'd marked with an adhesive tab. The drawing showed a heavily jowled man with a fierce mustache.

"This is Philip Crowe?"

Michael pulled a computer printout from his bag and laid it beside the sketch. The printout was a black-and-white photograph of a London society function. "See for yourself." He pointed to a man in the photo.

Leaning closer, Molly compared the drawing and the printout. "Kirkwell was a very good artist."

Michael smiled. "I thought it looked just like him myself. But it doesn't mean that Philip Crowe had anything to do with the robbery."

"It would be hard to explain what his image is doing in Kirkwell's book as often as it is." Flipping through the journal, Michael showed her other sketches of the man. They were all done in portrait style, illustrating Crowe without any background.

"If Philip Crowe were alive, possibly," Michael said. "But he's not. And any guilt might have gone into the grave with him."

"Maybe not." Keith shrugged. "My gran used to say you can't bury sin."

Molly turned a few more pages, then stopped at a drawing depicting the interior of a passenger car. It showed a young woman holding a child.

"Was Kirkwell on the train?" Molly's voice was cold and distant, and Michael knew she'd seen something troubling.

"Maybe, but we can't prove that sketch came from the Blackpool train." Michael had wondered the same thing himself. It appeared after the drawings of Philip Crowe but before those of the train wreck.

"I would bet it did."

"Why?"

"Because, as you pointed out, Kirkwell had a very good hand for faces. May I borrow your computer?"

Michael passed it across and she powered the computer up. When everything was connected, Molly searched the Internet briefly. With a satisfied smile, she turned the computer toward Michael.

"That is Audrey Cloverfield at the time of the train robbery."

Peering at the black-and-white photograph closely, Michael had to concede that Kirkwell's drawing might well have been Audrey Cloverfield. The girl looked young and innocent in the photograph as well as the sketch. Three necklaces—one with a cross, one with a silver rose and one with a flower pendant—hung at the hollow of her throat. It pained him to think of what the teenager had gone through at such a tender age. He couldn't imagine dealing with something as horrific as the train wreck at sixteen. He wouldn't want to deal with it now.

"I guess the three necklaces were a fashion statement?" Keith tapped the picture with a forefinger.

Michael shrugged. "Or it was safer to keep them close at hand in case she got separated from her luggage."

"Why would Kirkwell have been on the train?" Molly stared at the image in the journal.

"The robbers would have needed someone as a spotter," Keith said. "Could be some of the blokes stayed on the train to see if anything got changed up. They could have got off at the station before Blackpool, or jumped from the train shortly before it derailed. Might have been Kirkwell."

Molly took the photograph she'd lifted from Audrey Cloverfield's flat and placed it on the table. "Why would Audrey have taken a picture of someone in Blackpool? I would think after the train wreck that she wouldn't ever want to be reminded of that town again."

"What happened to her after Chloe Sterling died?" The possibility that the sketch of the young woman and child in the train car was that of Audrey Cloverfield and her unfortunate charge lent a somberness to the page.

"From what I read, she was kept on by Richard Sterling till he died, then she was let go. She continued working as a nanny for the rest of her life. Never married. Never had children."

"So this couldn't be her child?"

"No."

Michael studied the picture of the little girl with its backdrop of Blackpool Bay and Glower Lighthouse. "Evidently she meant something to Audrey Cloverfield. I don't suppose there's a date marked on this? Or that there was any reference in the book where you found it?" He turned the picture over and gazed at the blank surface.

"There wasn't."

"Unfortunately kids have a tendency to grow up and look much different than they did when they were young. She could be anybody."

"No." Molly shook her head. "That little girl was someone Audrey Cloverfield cared about—or else why keep the picture all these years? And Audrey had never been to Blackpool until the day of the train robbery. She didn't stay. She returned to London with Chloe Sterling's body."

"That wouldn't leave much time to meet someone in Blackpool."

"Unless she met someone on the train who meant something to her."

RAIN SWEPT IN FROM THE SEA and fell over Blackpool in blinding sheets. Hunkered under the eaves of the old railway station, Michael watched and cursed the unwelcome weather. His waterproof poncho and boots protected against the downpour, but the cold bit uncomfortably close to the bone. He was still tired from the long trip back from London last night. He'd tried in vain to get Molly to stay in the city, but she was anxious to return to Blackpool and work on salvaging the documentary.

Accepting the misery he'd chosen for himself, Michael turned to Clive Edgars and his brother, Neil. Both of the young men wore ponchos that matched Michael's as well as high boots. Unlike him, they both had beards and long hair that made them resemble pirates fresh off their ship.

"Big blow, ain't it?" Clive grinned, exposing white horselike teeth.

"Maybe there would be a better day we could do this." Michael didn't want to, though. Since returning from London last night, he'd become anxious to find some of the local spelunkers and tunnel rats to explore the caves and passageways around and under Blackpool.

"What?" Neil lifted shaggy blond eyebrows. "And miss out on all the atrocious weather? Perish the thought." He and his brother laughed as if it was the funniest thing they'd ever heard.

The two Edgarses operated a machine shop and salvage

down on the docks, but on weekends and evenings they crawled through the guts of Blackpool. Their father had done the same thing, and his father before him. All of them insisted that pirate treasure remained lost somewhere in the labyrinth below the town.

The treasure was a popular legend, and people had a choice of tales to pick from. The haunted walks put on by Other Syde Tours promoted such stories.

"Besides, water running in the tunnels might help expose hidden places, which is what you say you're searching for." Clive nodded toward the hillside where an opening lay. "Just have to be careful, is all."

"Don't want to end up drownt." Neil grinned at Michael. "Not that we'd let that happen to you, but flash floods can be a problem."

"Brilliant." Michael shook his head.

"If we don't go today, it's gonna be a week before we can play guide again."

"Okay. Let's do it." Michael took a deep breath and considered what faced him. He'd been underground in the tunnels before, but not with rainwater flooding the area. The possibility of drowning was distinctly unpleasant and one of his top fears.

More than anything, though, he wanted Molly safe and sound, and for all the lingering threats to vanish from their lives. In order to do that, he had to solve the mystery of the train robbery. Or convince her—and himself—that a solution after so much time simply wasn't possible.

He didn't know who would like that answer least. Molly or him.

When the Edgars brothers took off, Michael followed. The muddy ground sucked at his boots and filled the treads with clumps of grassy earth. At the hillside opening, Clive switched on his headlamp and swept an arm out to clear the brush and roots. Bugs and worms slithered through the loosened soil.

Absolutely lovely. Michael switched on his own torch, adjusted his backpack, and plunged into the deep throat of the earth.

CHAPTER TWENTY-SEVEN

ENOUGH RAINWATER HAD SLUICED into the passageway to make the footing treacherous. Michael slipped and tripped a few times, banging off the muddy walls before he regained his balance. The two brothers seemed as surefooted as mountain goats and talked incessantly about the past week at the docks. They cracked jokes and related humorous incidents with customers and tourists.

They also pointed out the sights to Michael: rocks that Neil felt certain had been shaped by Roman tools, an arrowhead that belonged to an English longbowman, shattered bits of pottery that must have already filled various collections, and other fragments no one had thought valuable enough to take.

Michael had gone spelunking with the brothers before and had enjoyed it. The Edgars were animated and knowledgeable, and extremely passionate about what they did. The hardest part of the experience was keeping up with the pace and the rapid nature of their conversations.

The tunnels under Blackpool were another world. The pirates and the locals had taken advantage of the natural caves that honeycombed the area, but in several places scars marked walls where openings had been enlarged with tools. Ground water seeped from the surface down the walls and contributed to the brown slurry illuminated by the headlamps. As the tunnel went deeper, the slurry gained speed and the rush of water became more audible, echoing in the enclosed space.

Choking down on the primitive fear that awakened in him, Michael focused on finding an underground passage the train robbers might have used. No matter how else he'd tried to envision the robbery, he'd returned again and again to the simple conclusion that the evacuation of the stolen goods had to have taken place underground.

The tunnels hadn't been explored much back in those days. People must have known about pirate treasure, but townsfolk hadn't wanted to venture into the tunnels. There were too many tales of curses and vengeful ghosts.

And there's always the possibility of a cave-in. Michael wished that thought hadn't occurred to him, especially when the tunnels were hemorrhaging rainwater.

He forced himself to continue on, focusing only on Molly and the danger she might be in.

Some distance farther, after several twists and turns that made Michael nervous about ever finding his way out of the maze of tunnels if he got separated from the Edgars, Clive stopped and shone his torch on a map he retrieved from his pocket.

"Should be near the train tracks where the robbery took place." Clive folded up the map and put it away. "Got to say, mate, you shouldn't expect much. There's been a lot of people passed through these tunnels since 1940."

Michael doubted that. Maybe a lot by Clive Edgars's standards, but only hardcore spelunkers would have come so far underground. Especially once it was established that no treasure existed in this area. Besides, those other explorers had been searching for treasure, not secrets.

"What are we looking for?" Neil shone his light around the dead end.

"Any point of exit would be wonderful." Michael slipped

a thin crowbar from his backpack and stabbed it repeatedly into the walls. The sharp end sank into the muddy earth several inches. Clods tumbled to the ground.

"Careful." Clive stepped back from the resulting splashes. "You do too much damage with that thing, you could bring the roof down on us. Today wouldn't be the day for that."

"I need to check for walls. A door. Something." Frustrated, Michael examined the wall more closely.

"You can still use that tool, just be more careful with it. How wide would the opening have to be?"

"Six feet. Eight feet. They would have had to truck the gold bullion out of here on some kind of cart." Michael was certain about that. "You're sure there's no other passageway around here?"

"None we've ever been in, and we've been in them all. This one was originally used to carry coal from the train to the houses in the area."

"To the Crowes." Michael dropped the end of the tool into the mud.

"Them and other folks, yes. Ain't just the Crowes living up in those hills, mate." Neil hunkered down in the muck, then gazed up at his brother. "How close would you say we are to the tracks?"

Clive shrugged. "Ten feet or so."

An image of the derailed cars filled Michael's mind. "The train cars were scattered during the wreck. The robbers would have had to allow for that. Wherever they broke through would have to be several feet from the track."

The Edgars retraced their steps and Michael followed. They played their torch beams over the ceiling. Michael did the same and sometimes caught rainwater in his face for his trouble. He spat out mud and had to rinse his mouth with water from the bottle he carried.

Nearly a hundred feet from the train track, Neil came to a stop and peered up. Tentatively, he reached overhead and scratched at the roof.

"What do you have?" Clive stood beside him and added his beam.

"Rock. Plenty of it. Strange we ain't noticed it before." Neil kept picking at the earth around the rocks, exposing more and more of the surface.

"Not strange. We weren't looking overhead."

Michael joined them and surveyed the roots thrusting through the cracks between the rocks. "The way it's overgrown, I'm surprised you noticed it now."

"Probably wouldn't have if it hadn't been leakin' so bad." Neil dragged a finger along one of the stones. "An' see here. This stone ain't natural. Not from around here. And it's cut, not rounded or odd-shaped."

Michael's excitement grew as the stone's true shape emerged from the dirt.

"An' here's where timbers have rotted." Clive dug splinters from fragile wood on either side of the tunnel. "Looks like those blocks were braced up in there at some point."

For a few more minutes, they worked together, gradually exposing a four-foot by six-foot section of cut stones supported by timbers and metal pipe.

"Somebody cut themselves a hole here." Clive hunkered down and drank from his canteen. "Might have been the train robbers, might not have been." He glanced at Michael. "Ain't no way of knowing now."

"Took care to cover it up, too." Neil glanced around. "Might be why the police didn't catch up to the robbers that day, but somebody should have discovered tracks or something in the next few days. Folks have always come down here poking round."

"They must have accessed another tunnel." Gold-laden

carts would have left deep ruts in the earth that would have been easily noted. He shone his torch on the ground. "Maybe a cave under this one?"

"Gimme your stick." Clive held out a hand and Michael surrendered the tool instantly. Carefully, Clive examined the walls, then chose the one on his left. He drove the tool into the earth, then heard it *thunk* dully. A grin split his face.

Without a word, Michael joined the Edgars brothers in tearing at the wall. In short order, they revealed a stone wall buried under a thick layer of earth. Only it began less than two feet from the bottom of the tunnel.

Clive and Neil took folding shovels from their packs and started digging. Clumps of wet earth thunked into the muddy floor, then they were able to start extracting the stones. Michael helped shift and stack them against the back wall.

"They didn't have time to dig this the day of the train robbery." Clive beamed his light into the tunnel they'd uncovered that lay next to the one leading to the Blackpool train station. "Couldn't have dug this much before that train arrived, either."

"So this tunnel already existed." Michael peered into the dark interior of the newly revealed corridor. It was five feet lower than the one they were in. Only two feet overlapped.

"Yep. Probably another coal tunnel. Only somebody decided to close it down after the robbery."

Michael wiped mud from his cheek. "Someone knew this tunnel was here the day of the heist. The people that planned this didn't just happen on it."

"Where does it go?" Neil crowded in beside his brother.

"There's only one way to find out." Michael slid over

the edge, getting caked with mud, and dropped into the second coal tunnel. He shone the torch ahead of him and realized the tunnel sloped even farther into the earth. Or maybe it was only his imagination.

"Surprised nobody discovered this." Clive clambered in after him.

"I'm not." Michael adjusted his pack's straps and started forward. "When the train robbery happened, everyone was more concerned over the deaths. All those children. And the survivors had to be made safe."

"And there was a war on." Neil trailed at the end of their little expedition.

"The police believed the robbers had gotten away by boat or by car." Michael walked around a turn and kept going. His boots squished in the mud. "They didn't consider the robbers might still be in Blackpool."

As he walked, Michael was unable to let go of the thought that the Crowe family lived in the direction he was headed. The smell of the dank earth crowded in around him and his heart thundered in his ears.

A quarter mile farther on, as near as Michael could estimate from the steps he'd counted, the tunnel came to an end. A wall of mortared stone blocked their way.

"What do we do?" Clive stood beside Michael and spoke quietly, as if someone might hear him.

"See what's on the other side." Michael took out his folding shovel and hoped it would be enough to get through the wall.

"You realize you could be breaking into someone's home, mate." Neil sounded nervous, but excited at the same time.

"If I do, I have a few questions to ask them." Michael rammed the shovel's edge home and it bit deeply into the aged mortar. Chunks rained down across his boots.

"Brill." Neil unlimbered his own shovel and got busy, as well. "They still gotta catch us, don't they? An' me an' Clive have these tunnels memorized better than anybody else ever could. Gonna be a right race if that happens." He chuckled gleefully. "You'll need to stay up, Michael, if it comes to that."

For a long while, only the dulled thump of the shovels striking stone filled the tunnel. Then, gradually, the stone blocks started to shift. Michael grabbed one in his gloved hands and worked it free. After that, the wall came apart easily and they stepped into a stone cellar.

To the right was a bulky furnace that had probably been used back in the day to heat the large house overhead. To the right was a nearly empty wine rack. Spiderwebs hung throughout the room.

"I really fancied we'd be starin' down the barrel of a fowlin' piece when we come through that wall. We wasn't exactly quiet." Neil shone his torch around the cellar and walked over to the wine rack. He inspected the bottles briefly. "Nothin' much worth havin' here. Probably most of it's gone sour."

Drawn by his own curiosity about the house and fully expecting to stumble into the Crowe ancestral home, Michael crossed to the stone steps that led up to the main house. His footsteps sounded loud in the empty room.

"Michael." Clive called to him. "Maybe we shouldn't just show ourselves in everywhere."

"We've come this far. I can't go back without knowing where we are. You two can turn around if you want." Michael never broke stride.

Clive and Neil hesitated for a moment. "In for a ha'penny, in for a pound." Michael wasn't sure which of them had spoken, but they both came up the stairs after him.

At the top, the door was unlocked. That surprised

Michael and made him even more leery at the same time. He could be stepping into a trap—then attributed the fear to his overactive imagination.

On the other side of the door, he entered a kitchen, which was just as abandoned as the cellar. He turned to the Edgars brothers.

"How many houses are empty up on this hill?"

Clive shrugged. "That's a few, mate. Them what didn't want to live here just moved away. Sometimes they just couldn't bring themselves to sell the old places, or maybe the inheritance was written so they couldn't. But a lot of people over the years haven't taken to the rumors of ghosts—like the one at Ravenhearst—or curses, and decided to leave."

A few minutes later, Michael discovered that the whole house lay empty. Dusty white sheets covered antiquated furniture and old portraits hung on the walls.

He shone his beam on the portraits. "Recognize any of those people?"

The brothers shook their heads.

The shrill ring of Michael's mobile nearly made him jump out of his skin. Recovering, he fished his iPhone from inside his jacket and answered.

"Hello."

"Hello, Michael." Aleister Crowe's smug tone was unmistakable. "How are things over in Starkweather Manor?"

Michael remembered the house then. He and Molly had talked about it with the real estate agent who had shown them Thorne-Shower. They hadn't ever been inside of it. The original owners had moved out shortly after World War II, after Victor Starkweather had been arrested for stealing oil from supply ships. Starkweather had also been one of the men Oatfield-Collins linked to the robbery.

"Dismal." Michael walked through the French doors onto the open balcony overlooking the hilltop. Rain splattered his poncho. Across the distance he could see Crowe's Nest, the ancestral home of Charles Crowe and his descendents.

"I'd been told you were exploring the tunnels." Aleister Crowe stepped out onto the balcony on the other side of the woods. He held an umbrella overhead.

"You're very well-informed."

"I suppose you unearthed Starkweather's little secret."

"Maybe it wasn't Starkweather's secret alone."

Crowe laughed. "Why don't you send your companions on their way, then come round. You and I can talk, and I'll tell you the story of my grandfather's folly."

"Of course." Michael couldn't resist the offer, but he had to wonder why Crowe wished to speak to him now.

CHAPTER TWENTY-EIGHT

MOLLY SAT AT HER DESK and massaged her temples in a vain effort to rid herself of the pain that had plagued her all morning. She thought the discomfort might have to do with the rain and her sinuses. Sometimes they flared up during inclement weather. Then she pegged it on fatigue from staying out too late, or possibly from traveling at night to get back home. In the end, though, she acknowledged it was from stress. Things just weren't going well.

I should have listened to Michael. One night in a hotel room wouldn't have mattered. Breakfast in bed somewhere other than home had sounded terribly wonderful that morning.

Especially since she had practically gotten nothing done since then.

She'd made a few phone calls, but because it was the weekend, most of the people she needed to contact concerning the documentary were out of the office. Still, they would have messages and e-mails waiting for them when they returned to work on Monday. And a few of them might even respond sooner.

Monday would prove a turning point for the documentary. Molly still felt positive that she could find a new director quickly and get the filming back on track, and the story of the displaced children from London could be told. That was the important thing.

"Headache?" Iris walked into the room.

"Yes. I can't seem to get rid of it."

"Perhaps a glass of wine."

"This early in the afternoon and with the way things are going?" Molly shook her head and regretted it as the pressure shifted behind her forehead. "I doubt I could stop at one glass."

In front of the desk now, Iris scanned the white board Molly had put there. Several pictures and copies of sketches from Kirkwell's book were taped across the surface.

"I must say, you and Michael have made a good run at solving the train robbery."

Molly leaned forward and studied the pictures. "Yes, but the hardest person to work into this whole thing is Audrey Cloverfield."

Iris took a seat. "She was on that train."

"As Chloe Sterling's nanny, yes. But why would she be so important now? Why would someone feel the need to murder her?" Just mentioning that fact called up an image of the dead woman stretched out in her flat. Molly shivered.

"I'm sure there must be a reason. She was killed by someone who was afraid of her. Or of what she knew."

"And then there's the photograph of the little girl in Blackpool." Molly took a breath. "Is she familiar to you?"

Iris bent to study the photograph, then shook her head. "I've looked at this several times. I still don't remember Audrey Cloverfield. She is a child herself."

"Do you recognize the little girl?"

"No, I don't recall her." Iris glanced at Molly. "If you think the girl is from Blackpool, you could try to get school albums and go through those."

"I've already set it up with the library. I should have access to several of them on Monday. But it's a lot of photographs to sort through because I'm not certain what year that picture was taken. And there's no guarantee that I'll recognize the little girl from a school photo."

At that moment, the doorbell chimed.

"I'll get it." Iris stood. "Irwin is busy changing the oil in the car."

Molly got up herself and walked in front of the board. Something—some clue—was right there. She knew it was. She just couldn't put her finger on it. Frustration made her temples pound harder.

"You have a guest." Iris didn't sound pleased at the prospect.

Turning toward the entryway, Molly saw Synthia Roderick standing beside Iris.

"I tried to leave her at the door, but Miss Roderick insisted that you would see her." Iris frowned. "I pointed out that in proper circles—more *polite* circles—one should call ahead to arrange a meeting."

If she took offense at the older woman's bold criticism, Syn gave no visible sign. Instead, the young woman smiled radiantly.

"Hello, Molly." Syn strode casually into the room and surveyed the white board.

"Hello, Syn."

Quietly, Iris walked past Syn and claimed one of the chairs in front of Molly's desk, then sat with an irritated expression and her arms folded.

Like a chaperone. Molly struggled not to laugh.

Syn's full-wattage smile never wavered. "I hoped we could chat alone."

"Iris and I were already involved in a discussion."

"Of course." Syn nodded to Iris. "I suppose my arrival is a bit rude and presumptuous."

"A bit." Iris's tone was as corrosive as hydrochloric acid.

"But I do have a good reason for being here." Syn reverted her attention to Molly.

"All right." Molly met the other woman's gaze full-on.

"I see you're working on the train robbery." Syn's eyes traveled over the white board, taking everything in. "Where did you get those sketches?"

"Michael turned them up."

"Fascinating. They're by someone who was at the train robbery?"

"We believe so." Molly glanced at the photographs again, but this time she focused on one of the necklaces hanging around Audrey Cloverfield's throat. The pendant was a small flower. Upon closer inspection, she saw that it was a rose.

The same rose necklace, or one very similar, hung around Abigail Whiteshire's neck in the group photo of the train robbery survivors.

And around the neck of the little girl in front of the Glower Lighthouse. Hadn't she seen it somewhere else...?

"You spotted the necklace, didn't you?" Syn's tone was casual, but Molly sensed an edge to the woman that hadn't been there before.

"What of it?" Molly didn't want to admit that she hadn't noticed the connection until just that moment.

With casual indifference, Syn took off her jacket and sat. She folded the jacket neatly in her lap, her eyes never leaving the pictures. "It was that necklace that got Simon killed. But I never understood why it was so important. Until now."

COLD AND WET, MICHAEL STOOD at the door to Crowe's Nest. He had parted ways with the Edgars, who'd wanted no truck with Aleister Crowe, and tramped across the woods separating the two manor houses.

Crowe answered the door himself. He was dressed elegantly as always. "Come in, Michael."

Michael indicated his wet clothing. "I'm not exactly outfitted for company."

"I'm prepared." Crowe indicated a runner of carpet stretched across the Italian marble tiles. "We'll talk in the library. Aunt Ophelia is expecting us."

"Your aunt?" Michael quickly reviewed what he remembered of the surviving Crowe family. Ophelia Crowe was the younger sister of Philip. She'd never married, though there was a lot of speculation about various men in her life when she'd been younger.

"Aunt Ophelia knows firsthand some of what transpired all those years ago." Crowe smiled coldly. "I...persuaded her it was in her—*our*—best interests to speak of the matter now."

"After keeping silent for seventy years?"

"She was only a girl at the time of the robbery. Hardly responsible for anything that happened then. Don't you agree?"

Michael wasn't certain of that, but he did want answers to the puzzle he'd been investigating for the last week. Molly needed to be freed of it. They needed their lives back.

"Lead me to your aunt."

"Great-aunt." Crowe crossed the grand room into the library.

The immense room held tall stacks of books as well as objects d'art. Vases and statues lined shelves and special niches designed for them. A suit of armor stood next to the door and leaned on a broadsword.

Ophelia Crowe sat in her wheelchair in the center of

the library, the couches and plush chairs flanking her on the Persian rug. A silver tea service sat on the low table in front of her.

In her early seventies, Ophelia looked like a resin model, not one white hair out of place, her makeup perfectly applied, her dark blue dress partially covered by the blanket over her legs, and her narrow eyes cold as marble. Time had withered her face and liver spots showed on her wrists where her white gloves ended. If she hadn't blinked, Michael would have believed she was the product of a taxidermist.

"Good afternoon, Mr. Graham." Ophelia didn't smile in greeting. "I'm told it's quite cold outside. Would you care for some tea?"

"As a matter of fact, I would." Inside the house now, Michael felt the chill seeping into him. He glanced around, then found one of the chairs had been covered by a water-resistant throw. The fireplace cast heat over him and he soaked it up.

Ophelia raised a hand and an older woman in servant's dress came forward to serve the tea. "Please sit, Mr. Graham." Ophelia waved to the covered chair.

Michael sat and tried not to seem as uncomfortable as he felt. Graciously, he accepted the tea from the servant and let the cup warm his hands.

"I'm told you found the coal tunnel to Starkweather Manor." Ophelia waved away the offer of tea, though the woman served a cup to Crowe.

Michael took a sip of the hot tea. "We did."

"We?" Ophelia shot a sharp glance at her grand-nephew.

"The Edgars brothers were with Mr. Graham when he made his discovery." Crowe didn't appear concerned.

"I don't like this, Aleister." Ophelia shook her head. "It's never good to have too many people know something that should never be known at all."

"Perhaps if my grandfather hadn't involved himself in the whole scheme in the first place, this wouldn't face us now."

Ophelia frowned sourly. "It's never wise to speak ill of the dead. I've advised you of that on several occasions."

"Because they might rise up against us?" Crowe raised a mocking eyebrow.

"Do not be so dismissive about powers you don't understand. You have not seen everything I have. The dead are never quite far from Blackpool. I have reminded you of this often, too."

"Of course. I beg your indulgence." Crowe didn't sound like he was begging, though, and his words had a sarcastic edge. "Maybe we should focus on what we have to tell Michael about the train robbery."

The old woman pinned Michael in her cold gaze and he suddenly had an image of himself as prey. "What have you learned so far?"

Michael hesitated for a moment, then decided to relate everything he'd uncovered. The Crowes wouldn't do anything to him, he was sure of that. The Edgars brothers knew Michael was there. And the Crowes wanted something, as well.

"I know that the train robbery was an inside job." Michael spoke calmly, but his heart was hammering. "The 'theft' of the paintings was originally an attempt to defraud the insurance agencies. That was a success. However, the people that owned the paintings were betrayed by thieves in their midst. Instead of giving back the originals, several of the pieces were replaced with replicas painted by a professional forger named Byron Kirkwell."

Crowe smiled. "You have been busy."

"Quiet, Aleister." Ophelia banged her fist on her wheelchair arm. "Let him speak." She shifted her attention back to Michael and nodded.

"Taking the gold along the highway or out to sea would have been hard." Michael shifted the tea cup in his hands. "The military was watching over the shipment. Not well enough, apparently, because they hadn't expected the level of treachery that the robbers were capable of."

The old woman's face blanched a little at that, but she held her tongue.

"If the robbers had taken the gold from Blackpool by car or by boat, they would have been caught. So they had to leave it here for a time. But they also needed a way to transport it from the train without leaving a trail for the military to follow. Once I learned of the coal tunnels that serviced the train and the houses out here, I assumed one of them must have been used. They could move the gold and art by mine car, the same as shuttling coal. Since no one had found the tunnel before, I thought maybe it had been covered over. It was." Michael looked at the two Crowes. "How am I doing so far?"

Aleister simply smiled and silently toasted Michael with his cup.

"My brother was a foolish man." Ophelia's voice was dry but strong. "Do you believe he was behind the robbery?"

Put on the spot, Michael shifted uncomfortably. "It's possible."

"Because he was the military liaison for the shipment. Because the men that planned the shipment lived here, at Crowe's Nest."

"Yes."

Ophelia snorted in disgust. "Then you're as much a fool as my brother was."

Michael shook his head and controlled his anger. "I don't

have to do all the thinking. I have enough to make a case for DCI Paddington. He can pull in forensic specialists to—"

"Muddy the water even further." The old woman cursed. "What we must do is solve the murders that have gone on this past week. Have you gotten so wrapped up in assigning blame for the robbery that you've forgotten those three unfortunates?"

"No." Michael didn't bother hiding his dislike of the woman anymore. He didn't care for her or for Aleister Crowe, and he didn't mind if they saw it. "I haven't forgotten them."

"Why were they killed?"

"To cover up knowledge of the train robbery."

"You're supposed to be a clever man, Mr. Graham. I'm disappointed. Why, after seventy years, would these people pose a threat? It will be hard to prove any of your conjectures. Harder still to reclaim anything that was lost that day."

"But perhaps not impossible."

Ophelia's lined features hardened with disapproval. "If you're not careful, you're going to let the real murderers get away with those crimes."

Michael forced himself not to point out that catching criminals wasn't his job. Still, his curiosity remained. "Perhaps you'd care to enlighten me as to what really happened."

"My brother was a pawn in the robbery for the most part. Victor Starkweather came to Philip and convinced him the gold robbery could be done, and that they could also profit from the insurance scam, as well. And so my brother agreed to it."

"For the money from the art or for the gold?" Michael kept his face impassive.

"Greed makes men reach for things beyond their capabilities, Mr. Graham. It's always been that way. Self-indulgence can bring even the best men down."

"So Philip Crowe hired Kirkwell to forge the paintings. Once the paintings were transported to Starkweather Mansion, it was probably a simple thing to exchange them for the forgeries he'd commissioned. Starkweather collected his insurance money, the others got what they thought was their art back and Philip and Starkweather sold the originals, the copies he'd had made and the art whose ownership couldn't be identified."

"Perhaps." Crowe wore that mocking smile again. "I seriously doubt that will ever be proved. However, for the moment, let's attribute both intelligence and avarice to my grandfather. Let us suppose he thought up his own wrinkle in the scheme to rob that train and found a way to get his hands on several of those valuable paintings and have forgeries made of them beforehand. But you have to wonder why the coal tunnel you followed led to the Starkweather house and not to Crowe's Nest."

After turning it over in his head for a moment, Michael nodded. Aleister Crowe was right about one thing: it would be hard to establish the story as truth.

"Take away the idea of the robbery, Michael. It's creating tunnel vision, so to speak, and we're losing sight of the murders." Crowe spoke quietly and confidently. "Open your mind to other possibilities. What else was lost in that train derailment? What else could be at stake even now after all these years? What secret yet remains stubbornly hidden? What would be worth killing over?"

"If you know, tell me."

Crowe shook his head. "If I had something to impart, I would have days ago when I first visited you and Molly. It would have been easier all around."

Michael went over everything that had happened over the last week. He kept coming up with one constant that neither he nor Molly could explain.

"Bartholomew Sterling is convinced that your grandfather defrauded his uncle of his paintings."

"Richard Sterling *was* defrauded. He was the one who owned those paintings. His brother Edward helped in the theft. Richard was a quiet man and not very trusting. Who do you think told my grandfather and Victor Starkweather about Richard's undeclared paintings? For a cut of the profits, of course."

"Edward Sterling knew your grandfather?"

"Of course. Philip Crowe was a friend of the Sterling family. A good friend."

"But still a thief."

A wry smile twisted Crowe's thin lips. "But still a thief. As was Edward Sterling. Bartholomew hasn't the right to be casting stones about the theft of the paintings unless he aims them at his father."

"Is he aware of that?"

"I believe so."

"Where are the paintings?"

"Would you believe me if I said I had no idea?"

"Not for a moment."

"Unfortunate, but that is my answer."

Ophelia spoke up in a more sedate voice. "As I said, Mr. Graham, my brother was a foolish man. Money found a way into his hands, and it quickly found a way out again. We were blessed that he had such a short life so that he couldn't squander the family fortune."

Crowe grinned at that, and Michael recalled how Philip Crowe had died in the early 1950s in an automobile accident coming down the mountain from Crowe's Nest. According to the newspaper reports, he'd been drinking at the time. Now Michael wasn't so sure.

Casually, Crowe sipped his tea. "Our family has a tendency to take care of its own mistakes."

Not a cheery thought. Michael was suddenly colder than ever. He put the tea cup down, then took out his iPhone and opened the photograph files he'd loaded into the memory. He bypassed several of them, stopping only when he had a picture of Edward Sterling.

The man was broad and beefy, with tightly kinked blond hair and malicious eyes. Still, he didn't look like the kind of man who would betray his brother. But if what Aleister Crowe said was true, and Michael didn't have any reason to disbelieve him, then he had.

But to what extent had Edward betrayed Richard?

Michael recalled everything he'd researched about the man. "Edward Sterling lived in his brother's shadow. The family money passed on to Richard because he was the oldest. Edward only had whatever money Richard gave him to live on. Agreeing to the robbery helped him feather his own nest."

"Exactly." Crowe nodded.

"But he didn't know about the forgeries your grandfather had made until much later."

"Edward Sterling obviously wasn't happy about that. If Grandfather had been alive at the time, I very much think Edward Sterling would have killed him."

"Richard wasn't in on the train robbery. Otherwise he wouldn't have let his daughter ride that train." Excitement thrilled through Michael as some of the pieces fit together in new ways. It was the same feeling he got when a game scenario started to fall into place.

Crowe nodded again. "Her death was unfortunate."

"Edward didn't warn his brother about the robbery, or

that the train would be derailed to occupy the military with helping survivors?"

"He probably assumed that his niece would survive. Or maybe he didn't realize she was going to be on board."

Michael clicked through a few more pictures and settled on one that showed Richard and Constance Sterling together at an event. Then he enlarged a portrait of the couple to check something that had caught his attention for the first time.

In the portrait, Constance Sterling wore a necklace. Michael enlarged the image again until he could see it more clearly. The pendant was a silver rose. It was the same silver rose he had seen Audrey Cloverfield wearing in Kirkwell's drawing of her, and the same silver rose the little girl was wearing in the picture Molly had found. It was also the same silver rose that had been on the cufflinks Bartholomew Sterling had flashed the day he'd met Michael.

Hurriedly, Michael pulled up the picture Simon Wineguard had been so interested in. When he blew it up, he saw that Abigail Whiteshire was wearing the same silver rose-shaped pendant. Or at least one very, very like it.

CHAPTER TWENTY-NINE

MOLLY STUDIED SYN RODERICK and hoped her excitement didn't show. Her mind wouldn't stop playing with all the variables, but she was certain that Syn couldn't have put together everything that Molly suspected. Otherwise the woman wouldn't be here now. *She's on a fishing expedition.*

"Why did you come here, Syn?" Molly kept her voice level.

Iris sat up a little straighter, but she didn't say anything.

Syn smiled. "I came here as a last-ditch effort to figure out Simon's secret. You know everyone involved in all this. I decided that if you hadn't figured out what his secret was, perhaps I'd never learn it, either."

"What secret are you talking about?"

Casually leaning back in her chair, Syn crossed her arms and regarded Molly defiantly. "I'd really hoped we wouldn't be playing games at this point."

"What do you mean?"

"I'm referring to the significance of the necklace that features so prominently in all those pictures on your board." Syn's eyes hardened, and for just a moment Molly was afraid of her. Then she pushed the idea from her mind.

"The necklace seems common enough." Molly's heart beat even faster.

"Does it?" Syn raised an arched brow. "Simon didn't think so."

"You seem to be more informed than I am. Do share."

Syn paused. "Simon was…quite reluctant to talk about the specifics of the matter to me. He lured me down here to this backwater town with promises of vengeance and riches. He said he finally had a way to get his revenge on Bartholomew Sterling for his daughter's death. And he claimed that we'd get a payday from it, as well. I was interested in the money, which is why I've funded certain ventures he's undertaken over the last year or so. Bartholomew Sterling has deep pockets."

Molly remained silent. She thought about the way Simon Wineguard's room had been methodically torn apart, and how his body had been deposited in the bin with a bullet in his head. And Molly thought about the number of people that could have gotten so close to Simon without sending him running for his life. Bartholomew and his bodyguard could never have done such a thing.

"Simon certainly didn't give me any details about any of this." Molly kept her voice soft, nonthreatening, but she wanted to warn Iris and get the woman out of the room.

"But you know about the necklace."

Molly shook her head. "I see the necklace in these pictures, but I don't get the significance."

Syn rummaged in her small bag. For an instant Molly glimpsed the hard metal outlines of a small silver pistol. Her throat dried and she would have bolted from the room if Iris weren't there. Then Syn took a picture from her handbag and handed it to Molly.

The photograph was of a young woman, perhaps in her twenties. She was beautiful and carefree.

"That's Constance Sterling. Do you recognize what's 'round her neck?"

Molly did. It was a silver rose pendant on a chain.

"I don't think Chloe Sterling died that day on the train." Syn spoke coldly and unemotionally. "Simon was going to give me the evidence. But then he became uncooperative."

When Molly turned over the photograph Syn had given her, she saw writing across the back. CONSTANCE STERLING, 1938. She recognized the handwriting as Simon's.

"Simon didn't give you this picture."

"Simon was an idiot."

"Did he just want the secret for himself? Or did he not trust you?"

Iris rose from her seat. "I should go check the roast in the oven."

Syn reached into her handbag and brought out the small silver pistol. "Sit back down, Mrs. Dunstead. Or I promise you, I will shoot you. I won't have you spoiling this by calling the police."

"Iris." Molly kept her voice calm with great difficulty. "Please do as she says. She killed Simon Wineguard."

For a moment Molly was afraid that Iris wouldn't sit. The older woman was quite capable of rebellion. Then Iris did as requested.

A mirthless smile twisted Syn's mouth. "You'll never prove that I killed anyone, Molly."

"Proving a murder isn't my job." Molly spoke calmly. "That would be the purview of DCI Paddington and his forensics people."

"I don't think they'll be quite up to the task, actually."

"Our testimonies might be worth something." Iris's defiance was like a naked blade gleaming with threat.

"With the barristers I have?" Syn chuckled confidently. "Neither of you would be a challenge to them."

Molly detested the confidence that the woman exuded.

But something else bothered her. "But you weren't responsible for Abigail Whiteshire's death."

"The woman killed behind the theater? The one Simon was convinced was Chloe Sterling all grown up?" Syn shook her head. "No. I was on my way to Blackpool at the time."

"She could have hired the men that killed poor Abigail." Iris glared at Syn. "It would have been no problem for her to pay a couple toffs to do the job."

"No. Simon wanted Syn here, but he didn't trust her enough to give her Abigail's name." Molly was growing more certain of her theory.

"Then who killed Abigail?"

"Someone else."

"Do you think so?" Syn smiled. "Personally, I wouldn't have put it past Simon. Maybe Mrs. Whiteshire wouldn't go along with him. Or maybe she wanted a bigger cut. Losing his daughter blinded Simon to many things, and it hardened him. He cared for very few people outside his own skin. When he discovered me in his hotel room, I was afraid he was going to kill me. But I was able to get him to follow me out to the alley. That's when he told me he'd gotten Chloe Sterling's identity wrong. It wasn't Abigail Whiteshire at all. But he refused to give me any more information and I realized he was going to cut me out of whatever scheme he had planned. I had crossed the line in his mind."

"Simon wasn't a murderer. He wanted revenge, but not at that cost."

"Are you so certain?" Syn's tone mocked Molly.

"Simon didn't try to kill you to protect his secret."

Syn smiled. "Perhaps, if this ever comes out, that would be a better way to deal with that particular situation. Self-defense. After all, Simon was quite beside himself with grief over his daughter, and he drank more than he should on several occasions. His toxicology from that morning will show he'd been drinking. I'll check with my barrister—if it should come to that."

"So why did you come to see me, Syn?"

"Because I still don't know who Chloe Sterling is." She adjusted the jacket in her lap. "Like you, I went in search of Audrey Cloverfield. I wasn't able to find her as quickly as you did. But I do have barristers that have a way to ferret out information that I want. I'll wager I know things about Miss Cloverfield that you don't."

Molly said nothing. She wished her mobile wasn't in her desk. She wished Syn hadn't brought a gun. She wished Michael was there, and just as quickly was glad that he wasn't.

"For instance, were you aware that Miss Cloverfield sent money to a barrister here in Blackpool every month after the train wreck?"

"No."

"Why, do you suppose, would Miss Cloverfield feel compelled to send that money?"

"You mean you don't know? With all those barristers at your beck and call?"

"Unfortunately, the one Audrey used has passed away and no one can quite remember where his records are." Syn shrugged. "Perhaps, if I had time, I could find someone to locate them for me. Unfortunately, I don't have time. You and Michael have kept pressing, and now—with Audrey Cloverfield's murder—the police investigations have intensified. So I came to you."

"You have more information than I do."

Syn shook her head. "Ah, but you can lead me right to Chloe Sterling."

"That little girl died on the train."

"No, she didn't." Syn pointed at the image of Audrey

Cloverfield on the train. "Miss Cloverfield is wearing the necklace there. She'd been hired by Constance Sterling to care for her child. At the time, Audrey had been more or less an orphan herself. She was raised by an alcoholic mother and very demanding grandmother by all accounts. Miss Cloverfield's ties to the Sterling family were deep. She continued to be Chloe Sterling's nanny even after Constance died."

"Then why would she hide Chloe Sterling in Blackpool?"

"Stop delaying! Take me to her. Three of those women were all adopted orphans from the train. I need to choose the right one, and I have precious little time."

"I'm not sure where to—"

Syn shifted the pistol over to Iris. "If you don't, I'm going to shoot Mrs. Dunstead."

"You wouldn't dare." Iris glared at the younger woman.

"Actually, I would. The economy has been unfriendly of late, and I've not been as careful as I should have with my investments. The money I can get from blackmailing Bartholomew Sterling would offset a great many of those losses." Syn shrugged. "Trust me. Getting off for murdering your friend—and you—would be much easier than dealing with the financial pressure I'm currently facing." She focused on Molly but she kept the pistol leveled at Iris. "Now what's it to be, Molly?"

"I'VE GOT TO GO." MICHAEL stood and put the iPhone away.

Ophelia Crowe looked confused and slightly miffed. "We haven't finished talking."

"And I say we have." Michael kept his voice firm.

"We need to come to some agreement, Mr. Graham."

"I believe we have, Miss Crowe. I don't care for you, and I doubt you care very much for me. For the moment, that suits."

Crowe stood, as well. "Where are you going?"

"Out." Michael left, squishing across the carpeted areas to the main door.

Long minutes later—too long—Michael opened the door of his Land Rover and slid behind the wheel. His breath ghosted out before him in rapid bursts from the awkward run through the woods back to the train station where he'd left his car. He'd fully expected Aleister Crowe to trail after him, but no one did. Maybe the Crowes were ready to concede their losses and be done with things.

The Land Rover started with a twist of the ignition and the thrum of the powerful engine vibrated throughout the interior. Michael slipped the vehicle in gear and drove a mile till he had reception on his mobile. He punched in Molly's number and got her answering service.

"Molly. It's me." Michael steered across the potholed back trail that led to the area where the robbery had occurred. "We have to talk. I know what's at stake. I know what Simon Wineguard was trying to discover." He shifted gears and gained speed. Mud from the spinning tires thudded against the tire flaps. "Chloe Sterling is still alive. Or was at some time. It's the pendant, Molly. That silver rose pendant that's in all the pictures. It belonged to Constance Sterling."

The Land Rover bottomed out in a small creek for just a moment. Michael fought for traction and kept going.

"That's what this is all about. If Chloe Sterling's alive, she's the rightful inheritor of the Sterling fortune. Not Bartholomew. That's why he's come sniffing around. Simon Wineguard must have threatened him with disclosing that."

Down in a small valley, Michael lost the mobile signal. He cursed and put the phone in the passenger seat, then concentrated on his driving as the Land Rover slewed dangerously near out of control.

It's all right. Molly is fine. Michael blinked as the windshield wipers fought with the muddy water that exploded up from the potholes. *Just keep it on the road.*

But the fact that Molly hadn't picked up when he'd called filled him with dread.

CHAPTER THIRTY

BEHIND THE WHEEL OF HER Mini Cooper, Molly surveyed her rearview mirrors hopefully. Rain relentlessly pounded Blackpool's streets, creating miniature waves across the cobblestones. There was no sign of Paddington's police escort.

Syn sat in the rear with her pistol. Iris sat in the passenger seat.

"What are you going to do with Chloe Sterling when we find her?" Molly cut her gaze to Syn in the mirror, amazed at how calm the young woman was.

"Offer her sanctuary, of course. I doubt Bartholomew Sterling would do the same."

Remembering the big man she'd encountered at Audrey Cloverfield's flat, Molly knew that was the truth. Bartholomew Sterling was a desperate man.

"How is protecting Chloe Sterling going to benefit you?"

"I'm sure we can come to an arrangement. After all, I'm in the position to make her a very wealthy woman. No matter what, she's going to need a top-flight legal team to fight for the Sterling fortune. I can provide that."

Molly couldn't help imagining Syn simply handing Chloe over to Bartholomew Sterling for a finder's fee. The possibility made her sick.

"Don't worry about that woman's safety." Syn waved

her pistol nonchalantly. "You should be more concerned with keeping Mrs. Dunstead and yourself alive."

Iris remained calm, her hands in her lap. "Do you really think you could get away with shooting us?"

"If I have to, yes. I do hope it doesn't come to that."

Molly didn't trust Syn. She didn't see any way out of the situation that would let Iris and her emerge unscathed. She only prayed that their destination would offer a chance for escape.

DRIVING THROUGH BLACKPOOL, Michael grew frustrated. He'd rung Molly's mobile and the house phone, then Iris's mobile. Finally he'd reached Irwin. From the sound of his voice, Michael assumed the man was in the manor house garage.

"Where's Molly?"

Irwin answered factually. "I'm not certain, sir. She and Mrs. Dunstead left with Miss Roderick a while ago. She didn't say where they were going or when they might be back. Is something wrong?"

Michael sped through the streets, narrowly avoiding pedestrians and bicyclists. Thankfully the rain had cleared most people from the town. His tires shrieked against the wet stones as he cut the corners tightly. The transmission protested as he shifted again and again.

"Yes. I don't have time to go into it now. Go out to the marina. Find Syn Roderick's boat. See if Molly is there. Then call me."

"Yes, sir."

Glancing at his phone again, Michael punched in the number for the Blackpool Police Department and got a dispatcher. He identified himself and asked to be forwarded to DCI Paddington.

"Mr. Graham?" Paddington sounded quiet and controlled. "Where are you?"

Michael powered through an intersection and barely missed a cyclist and a group of students hurrying toward a pub. "My wife is missing. She and Iris Dunstead left the house with Syn Roderick. I don't think Molly left by her own choice."

"Calm down, Mr. Graham. We'll get to the bottom of this. I need you to come here, to the police department. We can discuss it."

"Not till I find my wife. There's more going on than what you're aware of."

"Perhaps you could fill me in."

"Chloe Sterling is still alive, Inspector." Michael stomped on his brakes and skidded for a moment, giving a panicked cyclist just enough time to get clear of the intersection. Then he applied his foot to the accelerator and the Land Rover once more gained speed. "Audrey Cloverfield identified another dead girl as Chloe Sterling."

"Why would she do that?"

"Edward Sterling, the baby's uncle, was greedy. He knew the train was going to be robbed. Maybe he decided to seize the opportunity to get rid of Chloe and take control of the family fortune. Miss Cloverfield must have known this and protected the child as best as she was able. So she identified another orphaned child during all the confusion."

"Edward Sterling was behind the train robbery?"

"He was one of the men behind it. Victor Starkweather and Philip Crowe were also involved."

"Can you prove any of this?"

"That's not my job, Inspector. I've got some evidence. You'll have to talk to a prosecutor to figure out if it's worth showing in court. In the meantime, I have to find my wife."

"I just got a phone call from DCI Smollet in London. They arrested the man that attacked Mrs. Graham at Miss Cloverfield's flat. He was still marked by the pepper spray when they brought him in. He's talking to Smollet, saying he was hired by Hershel Conway."

"Sterling's muscle."

"Yes. The man Smollet has in custody is also talking about Conway running down another fellow named Byron Kirkwell in London a week ago. Do you know anything about that?"

"As a matter of fact, I do. Kirkwell was the forger Philip Crowe used to replicate the paintings he stole."

"I was about to contact you and your wife when you called. You should come here."

"Molly first."

Michael broke the connection and thought about the seven—no, *six*—survivors from the train wreck who lived in Blackpool. Two were male. One was Iris. That left three women. He thought fiercely, trying to remember their backgrounds.

You're looking for someone that was adopted. Someone whose parents died in London.

Then the name came to him. He called Information, gave the name, and asked for her address. When he had it, he punched it into the GPS program on his iPhone, his foot pushing down on the accelerator even harder than before.

THE HOUSE SAT BACK IN the woods outside Blackpool. Under the eaves of the heavy oak and elm trees, the single-story bungalow looked rustic and almost a part of the forest surrounding it. A narrow driveway trailed between trees and brush.

The ruins of Ravenhearst Manor lay only a couple miles

away. Most of the townsfolk avoided the area because it was overgrown and one of the local cemeteries was nearby. Teens often came out to the graveyard to drink and scare each other, and stories had sprung up regarding the ghosts of Emma Ravenhearst and Charles Dalimar, both of whom were said to still walk the manor house grounds.

"Pull up to the house and get out." Syn met Molly's eyes in the rearview mirror. "If you try anything, I will shoot you."

"Won't that be hard to explain?" During the drive, Molly had boxed away some of the fear that threatened to overwhelm her.

"You won't be here to care."

Molly eased her car into the drive in front of the house and switched off the engine when Syn instructed her to.

"The keys." Syn held out a hand and wiggled her fingers.

With a show of reluctance, Molly handed over the keys. She kept a spare under the rear wheel well, and though she hadn't checked it in months, she believed the magnetic keycase would still be there.

But even if she got away, bringing the other two women with her would be difficult.

Syn put the keys in her jacket pocket and motioned with the pistol. "Let's go meet Richard Sterling's legitimate heir."

With true reluctance and a feeling that she'd betrayed the woman, Molly climbed out of the car. At Syn's command, she halted at the front of the vehicle and waited for Iris to join her. Together, they headed toward the door.

Before they reached the house, the door opened and Rachel Donner stepped out, an apron tied around her. She dried her hands with a paper towel and looked uncertainly from Molly to Iris.

"Good afternoon. Did I forget you were dropping by?"

Molly shook her head. "Not at all, Rachel. Something came up that we needed to talk to you about."

"It would be better if we could discuss it inside." Syn stepped up to Molly's side and jammed the pistol into her back.

"Of course." Rachel retreated into the house.

Once inside, Syn moved away from Molly and revealed the pistol.

"What's going on?" Rachel's eyes grew round with shock. "Molly?"

"Sit down." Syn pointed at the chair and sofa in the modest living room. A soap opera played at low volume on the small television in the corner of the room. "I don't have a lot of time here."

Molly sat on the couch and was joined by Iris. Without taking her eyes off of Syn, Molly spoke calmly to Rachel. "You let Abigail Whiteshire borrow the rose pendant for the photo shoot for the documentary."

"Yes," Rachel said. "That pendant was one of Abigail's favorites. But what does that have to do with anything?"

"That pendant belonged to Constance Sterling, Richard Sterling's wife and Chloe Sterling's mother."

"Chloe was one of the children who died during the train wreck."

"Only she *didn't* die that day." Molly kept her voice neutral, wondering what Syn was going to do.

The young woman scanned the living room, then walked toward the curtains. Keeping the women covered with her pistol, she tugged at the cords and yanked them free. She tossed one to Molly. "Tie your legs together at the ankles."

"What if I don't?"

"Then I'll shoot you and ask Mrs. Dunstead to tie her ankles together."

Tires crunched on fallen branches and loose rock out in the driveway. Syn peered out the window and cursed. Through the sliver between the curtains, Molly spotted a luxury sedan pulling to a stop beside her Mini Cooper. Car doors opened, then closed, and footsteps sounded on the porch in front of the house.

Hershel Conway, Bartholomew Sterling's bodyguard, stepped into the room with a large gun in his very large fist. He glared at Syn as she wheeled on him with the pistol. Despite the gun aimed at him, he grinned.

"Gotta warn you. I don't have a problem shooting women." Conway pointed his weapon squarely at Syn.

At his side, another man Molly didn't recognize stepped into the room. He also pointed a pistol.

"Syn, I do believe you're outgunned, and in the interest of lessening the possibility of harm coming to anyone here, please reconsider what you're doing." Cautiously, Bartholomew Sterling eased into the living room, but he made certain he stood behind his bodyguards. "Do we have an agreement? I'd hate to have you killed."

Cornered and fearful, Syn backed away and aimed her pistol at Rachel Donner. "Don't take another step, Sterling. If you do, I swear I'll kill her."

CHAPTER THIRTY-ONE

WHEN HE SAW THE LUXURY SEDAN parked in front of Rachel Donner's house, Michael cursed and drove another fifty yards down the road. That distance put him around a bend in the road and out of sight from the house. He pulled off to the side, left the keys in the ignition and the engine running, and went to the trunk of the Land Rover. He opened the rear compartment, then felt inside the tool box until he found a tire tool. He expected to hear the crash and thunder of gunfire at any moment.

Turning, he raced back toward Rachel Donner's house, trying to stay out of sight. His brain spun as he figured out what he was going to do. So many people were inside the house, and there was no room for error.

In seconds, heart pounding from adrenaline as well as the exertion of running, keeping to the edge of the forest, Michael made his way to the front of the house. He spotted Bartholomew Sterling standing behind two men. One of them he recognized from their earlier meetings.

Trotting to the side of the house, Michael noticed that the curtains had been yanked from one of the windows. He flattened against the house and peered through the window. Molly and Iris and another woman sat on the couch. Syn Roderick had a small pistol pointed at Rachel Donner.

Staying out of sight of the two armed men and Syn, Michael waved at Molly and caught her attention. For a moment he thought she was going to give him away, then she caught herself.

Go to the rear of the house. Michael mouthed the words twice and watched as Molly gave him a slight nod. Heart thumping at the back of his throat, he crept around to the front of the house.

"Don't take another step, Sterling," Syn threatened in a loud voice. "If you do, I swear I'll kill her."

Michael got a fresh grip on the tire iron, rounded the corner, and stepped lightly onto the porch.

"Go ahead, Syn. Shoot her. It will save me the trouble. If I'd had any luck at all, the first woman I'd have killed would have been the right one. Better still, Audrey Cloverfield wouldn't have hidden the fact that Chloe was alive. My father had paid Audrey to make sure Chloe died on the train. But she betrayed him and hid Chloe in Blackpool. Only she couldn't go to my uncle with what she knew. Richard Sterling was too caught up in his grief over losing his precious wife. He depended on my father, but Richard was going to leave all his wealth to his daughter. My father wasn't going to let that happen. Now, thanks to Mrs. Graham, I have found the real Chloe Sterling and can put an end to any threat to my possessing the Sterling fortune." Bartholomew Sterling laughed. "That would have probably made an even better story for you, Mrs. Graham."

Dry-mouthed and scared, Michael swung around the corner with the tire tool. At the same time, Syn pointed her weapon at Sterling and started shooting. A rapid *pop-pop-pop-pop* split the air. One of the bodyguards sagged but Hershel Conway aimed his weapon and fired three quick shots.

Desperate, Michael hit Sterling from behind and knocked him into the wounded bodyguard. Both of them fell, sprawling to the floor. Blood leaked from the bodyguard and Sterling squalled for help.

Syn bounced off the wall behind her, then fell forward onto the floor as Hershel Conway swung around and pointed his pistol at Michael.

MOLLY YANKED IRIS AND RACHEL to their feet as soon as Syn changed her target to Sterling. Both women moved with astounding alacrity toward the rear of the house.

"The back door!" Molly followed as gunshots crashed behind her. She fully expected to feel bullets ripping through her body at any moment. But they didn't. She followed Rachel Donner through the kitchen and into the utility room, then out the rear door.

Behind the house, a short yard had been carved from the wilderness. Molly ran after Iris and Rachel as gunfire blasted behind her.

Michael!

CONWAY'S HASTE SAVED MICHAEL. The first couple rounds tore through the doorjamb a few inches over his head, splintering wood and filling his ears with cottony numbness. Then he recovered from his temporary paralysis and threw himself from the porch.

Frantic, Michael ran into the woods after the women, spotting them through the trees. He reached them in seconds.

"Keep going. They'll be coming."

"My car is there. I have a spare key." Molly touched his face, making certain he was all right. Her fingertips came away wet with blood and Michael guessed that the splinters had found a target after all. Thankfully nothing had hit him in the eyes.

"No." Michael pointed through the woods toward the

road where he'd parked. "That way. My car's already waiting. The keys are in the ignition. Get Iris and Mrs. Donner up there."

"Michael—"

They were still close enough to the house that Michael heard Sterling yelling invectives inside. "Find them! I want them dead, Hershel! Do you hear me!"

"We don't have time, love." Desperation surged within him. "Get them to the car. I'll be along."

"You'd better be, Michael Graham." Molly headed off with the other women, guiding them through the forest until they disappeared in the trees and brush.

Good girl. Michael tried to pretend that his heart wasn't ready to explode from his chest. He found a tree large enough to conceal him just as Hershel Conway burst through the back door of the house with the big pistol in hand. A flush of renewed fear chilled Michael.

"Have you got them yet?" Sterling staggered through the doorway after Conway.

"No. Where's Harry?"

"Dead. Syn was a much better shot than I anticipated."

The big man growled and spat a curse. "Well, she won't be shooting anybody else."

Sterling pulled a handgun from inside his jacket. "We've got to find them, then we've got some cleaning up to do here."

"What about the police? They could be here any minute. It might be better if we cut our losses."

"No. I won't be cheated out of my inheritance. We will track them down and we will kill them. If the police had been called, they would have been here by now."

Michael silently cursed, realizing he'd missed his opportunity to alert Inspector Paddington. The only thing he'd been able to focus on was getting to Molly.

Brush cracked in the direction that Molly and the women had gone. The sound drew Sterling and Conway's attention immediately and the two men set off.

Quietly, Michael shifted through the forest on an intercept course. He couldn't believe what he was doing. Reflexes honed on paintball courses, soccer fields and rugby games lent him grace and speed. In seconds he reached a point ahead of Sterling and Conway.

Conway was in the lead, swiping to clear branches and brush from his path. Mustering all his strength, Michael swung the tire iron sideways and whipped it into the big man's ribcage. Bone cracked and a savage jolt traveled up his arm from the impact. He cried out himself from the pain and shock.

Conway went down, the breath driven momentarily from his lungs. Sterling pulled up in alarm, staring down at his fallen companion.

Mercilessly, Michael swung again, striking Sterling's gun arm and sending the pistol flying from his grasp. A pained yelp escaped the man as he staggered backward. Driven by fear and rage, thinking of what Sterling had planned for Molly, Michael went after him. The muddy ground tore loose underfoot and nearly sent him into a tumble. It did save his life, though, because Conway recovered.

The big man rolled onto his side with a pained grimace and fired. Rolling thunder reverberated throughout the forest and bullets ripped leaves and branches from the trees. Michael threw himself to the ground, losing the tire iron in the process, then turned and dived through the brush.

Fire seared Michael's leg, signaling that the last tumble

had badly sprained or torn something in his hip. His leg moved sluggishly and slowed him down. Panting for breath, he hurled himself through the trees as Conway continued to fire. Thankfully the pistol ran dry.

Glancing back, Michael spotted Sterling just as he found his pistol and resumed the chase. Struggling to stay on his feet, Conway switched out magazines in his gun and matched his employer step for step.

The tree trunk under Michael's hand shivered as a bullet rocketed into it. Splinters of white bark erupted in a sudden spray. Michael turned and ducked, feeling the pain in his leg pull at him, causing him to cry out. Then he pushed himself for as much speed as he could manage.

He hoped Molly and the women had reached the Land Rover by now. Surely they'd had time. And surely Molly wouldn't make the mistake of trying to wait for him.

Three more bullets cracked limbs overhead. Another dug at his heels and ripped a clod of muddy earth free of the ground. Then the trees started to thin as he neared the road.

He risked a look over his shoulder and saw that Sterling and Conway had both gained on him. The damage to his leg was holding him off his best speed. Michael cursed and tried to force his body to go faster. But it wouldn't.

Another pair of bullets whizzed by Michael's head. The road was just ahead of him now, but he couldn't see the Land Rover. A green Jaguar flashed by. The brake lights flared to life, then a powerful engine shifted into Reverse.

Seconds later, when Michael was only thirty yards from the road's edge, the Jaguar came to a stop in front of him.

Anxiety whipped through Michael. Was the car's driver

another of Sterling's men? Then, incredibly, Aleister Crowe opened the door and stepped out, a pistol in his fist.

"Get down, Michael. Now!"

Almost overcome by pain and knowing he couldn't have gone on much longer, Michael threw himself to the ground. Bullets cracked around him. The driver's side window on the Jaguar suddenly exploded and glass rained down onto the muddy ground.

Calmly, as if it were something he did every day, Aleister Crowe set himself, one arm under his pistol barrel as he faced the two men. Then he squeezed off shots in rapid fire.

Jerking his head around, Michael spotted Conway lying still on the ground. Sterling had two blood-red roses blossoming on his white shirt as he leaned against a tree for support. Then his knees went out from under him and he flopped to the ground.

Without expression, without pause, Aleister Crowe strode forward to the two men and kicked their weapons away. Conway lay on his back, his eyes open and sightless. Sterling moaned in pain and terror.

"Please. You've got to get a doctor for me."

"You'll get one sooner than you deserve." Crowe gazed down at the man without mercy. "And you'll probably bloody well live."

Struggling, Michael pushed himself up, surprised that he was still alive. His leg burned from the movement. He stared at Crowe. "Thank you."

Crowe nodded. "You're welcome."

"How did you find us?"

Crowe smiled and made no effort to put his pistol away. He held it easily in his black gloved hands. "I followed you. While you were running back to your Land Rover at the train station, I waited in my car. You were rather difficult to stay behind at times, but I managed." He eyed the two men on the ground. "Otherwise I don't think this would have ended as well as it did."

Before Michael could respond, sirens pierced the air. He leaned heavily against a tree, then spotted Molly sprinting through the forest toward him. She wrapped herself around him, eliciting a cry of pain, then struggled to support him.

"This is going to require a lot of explaining, love." Michael grinned at her despite the pain and kissed her forehead.

"That's all right," Molly said. "Between us, we have most of the story. Inspector Paddington might even give us a medal."

Judging by the inspector's stony face as he stepped out of his car into the rain, Michael shook his head. "I seriously doubt that, love. We're going to be lucky if the inspector doesn't decide to lock us up on general principle."

"I'm here because I was kidnapped at gunpoint," she protested. "That's hardly my fault."

Michael wasn't convinced the inspector would see it that way.

EPILOGUE

Two days later, Molly gave a press conference in the Blackpool Library. Several television networks and newspapers had followed the Chloe Sterling story.

At present, Inspector Paddington had the podium. "From what we've been able to put together, Edward Sterling conspired to murder his young niece. He threatened sixteen-year-old Audrey Cloverfield till she agreed that the child wouldn't survive the trip to Blackpool. Miss Cloverfield knew nothing of the train robbery that had been planned, and it was fortunate she wasn't killed as so many others were. When she discovered Chloe had survived the wreck, she identified another dead child as Chloe Sterling. Miss Cloverfield then made sure the child—who became known as Rachel Donner—was adopted by a good family, and she sent money to a barrister here in Blackpool to help provide care for the girl until she was eighteen. She feared that revealing to anyone that Chloe Sterling was still alive would sign her death warrant. Now, I'll be happy to answer questions."

Realizing Michael had left the room at some point and that Paddington would be glad to step into the limelight for a time, Molly went in search of her husband. She found him at one of the displays with a cup of tea.

His leg was in a brace, though the physician had said

that it was only until the inflamed tendon quieted, but he looked as he always did. Casual and preoccupied.

"Not dreaming of mermaids?" Molly gestured toward the open notebook computer on the chair near Michael. The monitor displayed some of Keith's latest artwork for the game, and Molly was glad to see that they were more appropriate to the game's G rating.

Michael grinned at her, moving his attention from the display. He took her into his arms and held her a moment before he kissed her. Michael nuzzled her and she thrilled to the touch of his goatee against her neck. "So how goes the press party?" he asked.

"It's going well. The inspector has a flair for showmanship that I wouldn't have guessed at."

"Is he having a good enough time that he'll stop scowling at us soon?"

"No. He's not having that much fun."

"Too bad."

"I feel very used, though. Simon Wineguard played up the angle concerning the lost treasure from the train robbery to draw everyone out. He set them off in the wrong direction, for the gold and the paintings, instead of for Rachel Donner/Chloe Sterling."

"I should have thought of that, too. Didn't make sense for him to encourage competition for the search. But he was just using it to cover up his own investigating."

"So where did the extra forgeries come from?"

"From Kirkwell. After the search for the train robbers died down, he was in desperate straits and made a few more copies from his notes. I found entries in his journal regarding those. He sold them slowly, taking care to parse them out."

Molly glanced at the display case and spotted the

miniature version of Blackpool under the glass. "What's this?"

"A model of Blackpool during Charles Crowe's day. I'm told he made it himself."

"With all the pirating he was doing at the time?"

"Even with." Michael returned his attention to the case.

"You're quite taken with it."

"I am." Michael nodded. "It's very accurate. Built to scale. Quite impressive actually. But I can't fathom why he would build it and have it preserved here."

"Ego. Men are generally known for their massive egos."

Michael held her and didn't say anything.

"A lot has changed since the model was built." Molly noticed the way some of the buildings now differed from what had been there back in the day.

"Situations change. Look at Rachel Donner."

"I know. I'm glad Bartholomew Sterling survived being shot, and I'm even more glad that no charges were pressed against Aleister Crowe. But now Sterling will see all of his wealth being given to Rachel. As it should have been. She has children, and now she has enough money to help them and her grandchildren. She's quite excited."

Michael glanced into the room being used for the press conference. "Are you required any further here?"

Molly smiled at him. "Not really. I'm sure the inspector can handle everything."

Grinning, Michael started pulling her toward the front door. "Did I mention that I packed a picnic basket this morning? With Iris's help?"

"No, you did not."

"And that it contained a bottle of your favorite fruit wine?"

"No."

"Or that I've found a perfectly secluded little beach that I can get to in my Land Rover?"

"I've not heard a word."

Michael smiled at her again as they stepped out into the morning sunlight. "Well then, it must be because it's all a surprise."

* * * * *

LARGER-PRINT BOOKS!

GET 2 FREE LARGER-PRINT NOVELS

PLUS 2 FREE GIFTS!

HARLEQUIN®
INTRIGUE®

Breathtaking Romantic Suspense

YES! Please send me 2 FREE LARGER-PRINT Harlequin Intrigue® novels and my 2 FREE gifts (gifts are worth about $10). After receiving them, if I don't wish to receive any more books, I can return the shipping statement marked "cancel." If I don't cancel, I will receive 6 brand-new novels every month and be billed just $4.99 per book in the U.S. or $5.74 per book in Canada. That's a saving of at least 13% off the cover price! It's quite a bargain! Shipping and handling is just 50¢ per book.* I understand that accepting the 2 free books and gifts places me under no obligation to buy anything. I can always return a shipment and cancel at any time. Even if I never buy another book from Harlequin, the two free books and gifts are mine to keep forever.

199/399 HDN E5MS

Name _____ (PLEASE PRINT)

Address _____ Apt. #

City _____ State/Prov. _____ Zip/Postal Code

Signature (if under 18, a parent or guardian must sign)

Mail to the **Harlequin Reader Service:**
IN U.S.A.: P.O. Box 1867, Buffalo, NY 14240-1867
IN CANADA: P.O. Box 609, Fort Erie, Ontario L2A 5X3

Not valid for current subscribers to Harlequin Intrigue Larger-Print books.

Are you a subscriber to Harlequin Intrigue books and want to receive the larger-print edition? Call 1-800-873-8635 today!

* Terms and prices subject to change without notice. Prices do not include applicable taxes. N.Y. residents add applicable sales tax. Canadian residents will be charged applicable provincial taxes and GST. Offer not valid in Quebec. This offer is limited to one order per household. All orders subject to approval. Credit or debit balances in a customer's account(s) may be offset by any other outstanding balance owed by or to the customer. Please allow 4 to 6 weeks for delivery. Offer available while quantities last.

Your Privacy: Harlequin Books is committed to protecting your privacy. Our Privacy Policy is available online at www.eHarlequin.com or upon request from the Reader Service. From time to time we make our lists of customers available to reputable third parties who have a product or service of interest to you. If you would prefer we not share your name and address, please check here. ☐

Help us get it right—We strive for accurate, respectful and relevant communications. To clarify or modify your communication preferences, visit us at www.ReaderService.com/consumerschoice.

HILP10R

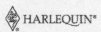